# Everyone Remembers The Play

*A Compilation of Five Reverently Humorous,*
*Soul-Searching Plays for Children, Youths, and Young Adults*

BARBARA PEART-JAMES

WESTBOW
PRESS
A DIVISION OF THOMAS NELSON

All Scripture quotations, unless otherwise indicated, are taken from the King James Version of the Bible.

Suitable for
- Main church services
- Camps
- Retreats
- Bible studies
- Bedtime stories
- Just about any occasion

WestBow Press books may be ordered through booksellers or by contacting:

WestBow Press
A Division of Thomas Nelson
1663 Liberty Drive
Bloomington, IN 47403
www.westbowpress.com
1-(866) 928-1240

ISBN: 978-1-4497-3165-6 (sc)
ISBN: 978-1-4497-3164-9 (e)

Library of Congress Control Number: 2011960654

Printed in the United States of America

WestBow Press rev. date: 11/15/2011

I would like to dedicate this book to my wonderful children, Phillip and Natasha. You always bring such vigor and veracity to each of the characters you have portrayed. Even from your tender ages, you understood how important it was to get each line just right, so the correct message would be received. You have forgone many hours of your play time in order to learn your lines, rehearse, and even edit these plays with me. For this I am so grateful. You have been my main actors in every presentation, always with rave reviews. Your enthusiasm and unwavering support for each play, from the inception, is just amazing. Although you are my biggest critics, you are also my chief supporters. Thanks for the inspiration, and I hope you'll always look back on your childhood as being a fun one, mainly because of your involvement in these plays.

To my nephew, Serdel, who presently lives with us, thanks for being so committed to the task when asked to perform. You certainly impressed everyone in your first performance when you learned so many pages of script in just under a week—and you just keep getting better.

Finally, to everyone who already has performed—or will read and perform—in these plays, it is my desire that you allow these words to help mold your Christian character, and that your lives will be more meaningful because of them.

# Contents

# Acknowledgments

First and most important, I would like to thank **God** for helping me to discover this talent, and also for providing me the help and forum in which to present these plays. My walk with Him has become much closer through writing these plays, and I know that He will continue to guide and direct my path, as long as I allow Him to.

To my husband, Patrick James, thanks for always being there to assist in whatever way you can—whether by suggesting how to rephrase a line, proofreading, videotaping performances, gathering supplies, or helping with the stage setup. It is comforting to know that I can count on your continued support, and my prayer is that we will keep growing in love, together in Christ.

To Frances Gotsis, thanks for operating in so many different capacities and for constantly helping. Your gift of creativity is just amazing! You are the brains behind these pictures, bringing the script to life. I pray that your unique talent will be discovered and your hard work will be rewarded. I hope that our relationship will continue to blossom as we strive to win souls for the Lord.

To Mancel and Joy Alexander, thanks for always lifting me up in prayer. You were among the first to suggest that I write a book of plays, and you frequently make yourselves available to advise, edit, and be sources of support.

To Carlton Foster, thanks for the tremendous support you have continually given. You spent numerous hours helping with technical difficulties and guiding me through Microsoft Word. You always make yourself available, whenever called upon, and for this I am extremely grateful.

To my friend and brother in Christ, Success St. Fleur, and my friends Leon Martin and Millicent Wynter, my thanks for your devotion to this project. To the rest of my coworkers, you have been a rich source of encouragement, and I thank you all.

To all my other well-wishers, thank you so much for your encouragement along the way. I do feel the genuine excitement, and I hope all of you will be happy with the final product, and pleased that I did take your suggestions seriously.

# 1

# The Prodigal in Me

## A Lesson in Forgiveness

"And he was angry, and would not go in: therefore came his father out, and intreated him. And he answering said to [his] father, Lo, these many years do I serve thee, neither transgressed I at any time thy commandment: and yet thou never gavest me a kid, that I might make merry with my friends:

But as soon as this thy son was come, which hath devoured thy living with harlots, thou hast killed for him the fatted calf.

And he said unto him, Son, thou art ever with me, and all that I have is thine.

It was meet that we should make merry, and be glad: for this thy brother was dead, and is alive again; and was lost, and is found." (Luke 15:28–32)

"What man of you, having an hundred sheep, if he lose one of them, doth not leave the ninety and nine in the wilderness, and go after that which is lost, until he find it?" (Luke 15:4)

"Either what woman having ten pieces of silver, if she lose one piece, doth not light a candle, and sweep the house, and seek diligently till she find [it]?" (Luke 15:8)

Grace is good news that God loves and cares for us—so much that He made us His children. Grace is God's gift of love, rescuing us from Satan. Because God loves us, He forgives our past mistakes and treats us as if we have never sinned. In this modern-day interpretation of the parable of the prodigal son, we will observe just that.

# CHARACTERS

BRO. BROWN  Recently returned to the fold after being away for many years. Looks like he needs some help; poorly dressed.

SIS. PERLA  Self-righteous and unforgiving. Modestly dressed with a hat and carrying a Bible.

SIS. JOYCE  Church sister who was also initially intolerant of Bro. Brown. Also modestly dressed.

BRO. PETER  The open-minded, objective church brother. Pleasant; wears a suit.

# SETTING

In the church parking lot, after midday service.

Later Sis. Perla is alone at home.

Following week at church, again after service is dismissed.

# TIME

Summer 2009.

# SCENE I

(Sis. Perla and Sis. Joyce are talking in the parking lot; Bro. Brown, the Prodigal, walks up to greet them.)

BRO. BROWN
(Happy and bubbly.)
It's so nice to see you two lovely ladies today. How are you doing?

SIS. JOYCE
(Smiling.)
Wonderful! How are you?

SIS. PERLA
(Keeps quiet, trying to ignore him.)

BRO. BROWN
(Full of joy and excitement.)
Oh, I'm just great! What a wonderful message; it touched every fiber of my being.
(Sighs, but then smiles; looks at his watch.)
Anyway, got to run.
(Wags his right index finger at them.)
You have a wonderful week.

SIS. JOYCE
Okay, you too.
(Smiling.)

SIS. PERLA
(Gives a plastic smile, but she is not speaking just yet.)

BRO. BROWN

(Starts to walk away, but then turns around, beams a huge smile, and cites Proverbs 17:22.)

"A merry heart doeth good like a medicine: but a broken spirit drieth the bones." So try to wear a smile on your faces.

(Turns around and continues to walk away.)

SIS. JOYCE

Okay, will do.

SIS. PERLA

(Watches him leave; keeps wearing a plastic smile until he is finally out of their hearing. She suddenly switches moods.)

Ha! We'll see how long *that* lasts.

SIS. JOYCE

(Surprised.)

Excuse me? … What was that?

SIS. PERLA

The Prodigal!

(Pauses, shakes her head, and smirks.)

Don't you remember how he was the hottest thing in here? He was so hot, the church could not contain him. So he left us—for more than twenty-five years—drinking, smoking, and partying with all those women.

SIS. JOYCE

(Thinking; trying to remember.)

Oh, yes, he thought he was so happy with lots of money and friends.

SIS. PERLA

You know, he didn't even talk to his family at one point.

SIS. JOYCE

Yes, and I heard that he didn't even take care of all those kids he has.

(Pauses.)

They're fully grown now; I hear they don't even speak to him.

**Ha, we'll see how long that last"**

SIS. PERLA

(Mockingly.)

So, now that the recession has caught up with him, he's broke. All his friends are gone, and he's returned to us—as if we have some of that stimulus money to give away.

(Both are now laughing. Bro. Peter walks up and starts talking to them.)

BRO. PETER

What's so funny, ladies?

(They both hesitate, looking at each other. No one wants to speak.)

BRO. PETER

(Prompts them.)

Come on. ... Make me laugh too.

SIS. PERLA

(Decides to speak.)

Well, it's Brother Brown. ... We're just saying that he spent all his youthful years with Satan, and now that he is all worn out, he's back.

SIS. JOYCE

(Her tone of voice debases him.)

God must be so disappointed! He does not want any tired body.

BRO. PETER

(Disagrees.)

Well, the Bible does say to come as you are, meaning, young or old, black or white, pretty or ugly, rich or poor, and tired or not.

SIS. PERLA

(Disappointed and sulking.)

It's not fair. He went away, looking for happiness and forgetting about God, while we have been here for so many years, fighting the good fight.

(Turns to Bro. Peter.)

So why should we embrace him?

BRO. PETER

Hey, remember what Isaiah 55:7 tells us: "Let the wicked forsake his way, and the unrighteous man his thoughts: and let him return unto the LORD, and he will have mercy upon him; and to our God, for he will abundantly pardon."

SIS. JOYCE
(Puts her hand over her mouth, thinking. Has a change of heart. Removes her hand and turns to Bro. Brown.)

I agree. Matthew 5:45 says, "….for he maketh his sun to rise on the evil and on the good, and sendeth rain on the just and on the unjust."
(Turns to Sis. Perla.)

It might seem unfair to us, but not to God.

SIS. PERLA

I know what you're saying, it's just that …
(She looks frustrated.)

BRO. PETER

Tell me, Sister Perla. … Why are you so upset with this man?
(He pauses, waiting for a response; when there is none, he continues.)

Is it because he went out there and "had fun," but got back in time?
(Now very direct and forceful.)

Or is it because you wanted to do that too, but you were just too afraid of what the other church members would say?

SIS. PERLA
(Shocked; opens her mouth; wags her finger at him, and shakes her head.)

Oh, no, you didn't!

BRO. PETER
(Teasing.)

Oops, you seem angry. You need to go see Pastor!

SIS. PERLA
(Even more upset.)

I don't need Pastor.

BRO. PETER
(Sympathetic.)
You're right. You need more than Pastor … you need Jesus!

SIS. PERLA

Oh really? I already have Him!

BRO. PETER
(Stunned.)

Really? Wow!

SIS. JOYCE
(Interjects, trying to understand Sis. Perla's feelings.)
I know. You feel like you have forgone the pleasures of sin; therefore, it would be wrong to forgive and embrace someone like him, right?

SIS. PERLA
(A little relieved and happy for the support.)
Yes, and each time I see him, he acts as if nothing had happened. And he's always so bubbly, as if he is still drinking some of that Jamaican white rum.
(She makes a drinking motion with her hand.)

BRO. PETER
(Soberly warning Sis. Perla; serious tone; cites Matthew 7:1.)
"Judge not, that ye be not judged."
(Smiling.)
Perhaps he is always so happy and bubbly because he feels that in spite of all that he has done, God still loves him and embraces him; and he finally …
(Elevates his tone.)
… finally has peace …
(Lowers voice.)
… perfect peace.

SIS. PERLA
(Thinking; speechless.)
Well …

SIS. JOYCE
*Hmmm!* Something to think about while I leave. … Bye, guys … see you next week.

SIS. PERLA
(Looks at Bro. Peter; quickly checks her watch.)

Wow! Where did the time go? I have to leave too.

BRO. PETER
(Smiling mischievously.)

Why? Is it getting too hot in here?

SIS. PERLA
(Displeased.)

Seriously?

BRO. PETER

Well, what else am I to believe? I really do not want us to part like this. Let's wrap this up, shall we?

SIS. PERLA
(Matter-of-fact and without looking at him.)

Yeah, yeah. … Bye, Brother Peter.

(Leaves the stage.)

BRO. PETER
(Speechless; stands watching her while shaking his head; he also leaves.)

# SCENE II

(Sis. Perla is alone at home. She sits down with her Bible to have devotions, but remains troubled about Bro. Brown.)


SIS. PERLA
(Visibly upset.)

God, why do You treat me like this? For thirty-two years I have been walking faithfully with You. I've watched as people come and go … turning their backs on You.

(Gets up and paces the floor.)

All these years I have kept things together and what do I have to show for it? … They come back and get the better positions and recognition, while I go by unnoticed.

(Pitying self.)

I feel so alone.

(Sits down again, still tormented.)

No one has ever given me a pat on the shoulder or even mentioned my name in their honorary services. It seems like I am always living in the shadow of all these people who have shamed You so badly. … So, I have to tell You, Lord, that I am really disappointed and tired of this.

(Frustrated, she takes the Bible and puts it aside; she leaves.)

# SCENE III

(Following week at church. Sis. Perla sees Bro. Peter and tries to avoid him, but he catches up with her.)

BRO. PETER
(Trying to get her attention.)

Sister Perla ... Sister Perla!

SIS. PERLA
(Reluctantly responds, without fully turning around.)

Yes, Brother Peter?

BRO. PETER

How are you? How was your week?

SIS. PERLA
(Clearly annoyed.)

I am fine ... and so was my week. How may I help you?

BRO. PETER

Do you have plans for lunch? 'Cause I would like to invite you to have lunch with me.

SIS. PERLA
(Flattered; smiling.)

Lunch! Today?

BRO. PETER
(Smiling.)

Yes ma'am.

SIS. PERLA

Sure. Um ... I'm vegetarian. I hope that will not be a problem.

BRO. PETER

Absolutely not ... that's been taken care of. I've done my homework.

SIS. PERLA

(Looks surprised; smiles.)


BRO. PETER

Excuse me for a few seconds while I give those folks the directions.
(Walks offstage; people hidden.)


SIS. PERLA

(Watches him go. Notices who he is talking to; starts complaining while shaking her head.)

Am I really supposed to sit and eat with those people … as if everything is just fine?
(Looks up.)

How long do I have to endure this, God? How long will You allow these people to ridicule You? … I need mercy, Lord … when are You going to show me some mercy?


BRO. PETER

(Returns to stage.)

Are you okay? I thought I heard you talking to yourself.


SIS. PERLA

(Suddenly finds an excuse to decline his lunch invitation.)

Ah … well … I was just … um … I don't think I'll be able to make it to lunch, after all.


BRO. PETER

(Now suspicious; looks in the direction of the other guests and then looks back at her.)

Are you still carrying grudges? … Come on, Sister.


SIS. PERLA

(Defensive.)

Well, at least I am not helping them to make a mockery of God!


BRO. PETER

(Surprised.)

What?

(Pauses, with his eyes on the ground while thinking; looks up and directly into her eyes.)

Okay. Let me ask you a question. Did you sin last week?

SIS. PERLA
(Shocked.)

Excuse me?

BRO. PETER
(Insistent.)

Answer the question, Sister. Did you?

SIS. PERLA
(Unsure of how to respond, she turns her head away from him before answering.)

Of course ... I ... I must have; no one is perfect.

BRO. PETER

How about yesterday?

SIS. PERLA
(Hesitates; speaks reluctantly.)

Maybe. ...

BRO. PETER

And today?

SIS. PERLA
(Upset.)

I don't know! Why are you grilling me?

BRO. PETER
(Ignores her question.)

Do you ask for forgiveness when you sin?

SIS. PERLA
(Composing herself, she appears somewhat calmer.)

Of course! I do that every day.

BRO. PETER

Do you feel like you're forgiven?

SIS. PERLA

(Very forceful and confident.)

Well, yes, of course. Jesus assures me of that. In Jeremiah 31:34 He says, "….I will forgive their iniquity, and I will remember their sin no more."

BRO. PETER

(Smiling.)

So, don't you get it? Sin is sin, and if you expect the Lord to forgive you, aren't you in return expected to forgive your fellow men?

Moreover, God forgives him whether or not you do, so … get over it.

SIS. PERLA

(Considers what he just said.)

Well, I see your point, but … *hmmm* …

(Clenches her teeth and closes her fists.)

… it's so hard to move on!

BRO. PETER

Those of us deceived by Satan look upon God as being scrupulous and unkind. We regard Him as watching constantly with the intention to rebuke and accuse. But …

SIS. PERLA

(She finally gets it; interrupting him by holding out her hand for him to stop speaking, she smiles and nods her head.)

Ah … yes! When we see ourselves as sinners, saved only by the love of God, we will have compassion for others who are suffering in sin.

BRO. PETER

(Ecstatic; jumps up joyfully.)

Amen, Sister Perla! I think you finally get it.

"Wow!
I was the lost coin!

SIS. PERLA

(Reflective.)

I claimed to be a child of God, but I was acting out the spirit of Satan.

(In a lightbulb moment she shakes her head.)

Wow … I was the lost coin!

(Clasps hands to pray; remorseful.)

O Heavenly Father, forgive me; all my righteousness is no more than filthy rags before You.

BRO. PETER

(Agrees.)

Exactly! Self-righteousness not only leads us to misrepresent God, but it also makes us coldhearted, judgmental, and unkind to one another.

SIS. PERLA

(Joyful.)

John 6:37 says, "….And him that cometh to me I will in no wise cast out." Yes, the blood of Jesus cleanses us all from sin.

BRO. PETER

Yes! When we ask God to forgive us, He does it instantly.

(Snaps his fingers.)

And then He blots it out of His mind. … He won't think of it again. Just think how happy God will be when you do that for others; and … you'll feel better too!

(Playfully mocking.)

Who knows? You might just become bubbly like Brother Brown.

(Both laugh.)

SIS. PERLA

(Faces the audience/congregation.)

Remember the Shepherd had ninety-nine other sheep, but he rejoiced so much when he found that one sheep that was lost.

(Pauses.)

So there will be a great party in heaven over just one sinner who repents, rather than over ninety-nine people who think they are so perfect that they do not need to repent.

(Warns gently but firmly.)

Don't be the lost coin!

(Turns to Bro. Peter and gives him a big hug.)

Thank you, Brother Peter. Thanks for showing me the light.

**THE END**

# 2

# Altar Fashion

## Modesty Is the Key in Christian Dress

"But ye are a chosen generation, a royal priesthood, an holy nation, a peculiar people; that ye should shew forth the praises of him who hath called you out of darkness into his marvellous light." (1 Peter 2:9)

"For ye are bought with a price: therefore glorify God in your body, and in your spirit, which are God's." (1 Cor. 6:20)

"It is good neither to eat meat nor drink wine nor do anything by which your brother stumbles or is offended or is made weak." (Rom. 14:21)

As Christians everything we do should bring praise to God. A practical way in which we worship Him is through our choice of dress. This play critically examines the way we clothe ourselves as Christians, in general, and especially when we enter into the house of the Lord.

# CHARACTERS

| | |
|---|---|
| BRO. PAUL | Playful; always hankering for the women. Sharp dresser; wears a suit. |
| BRO. MIKE | Sober, sincere, and self-controlled; wears a modest suit. |
| SIS. JESSIE | Liberal in Christian dress principles; showing lots of skin and cleavage. Dress is similar at the meeting. |
| BRO. CARLTON | The very open-minded husband who later becomes disappointed with his wife's outfit. |
| SIS. ROSIE | The irresponsible, resolute, self-absorbed wife; wears tight-fitting, revealing clothes. Later at business meeting she dresses quite modestly. |
| BRO. BARRY | Moderator for the business meeting; modestly dressed. |
| SIS. NANCY | Just another church member who is not concerned about the way she dresses; skimpily clad. |
| SIS. MONICA | Radical; wears clothing with long sleeves, high necks and ankle-length hems. |

# SETTING

The members are on the church premises, prior to service commencing. A church brother is outside amusing himself by watching the ladies go from the parking lot into the church. He is later joined by some other church brothers; they proceed to discuss the manner in which the members dress, in contrast to how they really should dress.

Later this problem is a hot topic for discussion during a business meeting.

# TIME

Midmorning, before service begins. Another evening.

# SCENE I

(A couple of women are walking from the parking lot to the church building. Bro. Paul, noticing them, is very excited.)

BRO. PAUL

(Rubs his hands together, talking to himself.)

Yes, let the games begin! Ha, ha … h-a-a-a … beautiful.

BRO. MIKE

(Walks up to Bro. Paul; looks a little puzzled.)

Hey, Paul … what's happening, bro?

BRO. PAUL

(Smiles and nods his head.)

Just enjoying the free show! Coming to church sure has some perks.

BRO. MIKE

(Confused.)

What? What are you talking about?

(A few women are now walking across the parking lot. Some are in revealing clothes—tight, short, skirts, and low-cut tops exposing cleavage and shoulders.)

BRO. PAUL

(Points to the women walking.)

Look!

(He is so excited, he almost sings.)

Do you see what I see? Wow! Showers of blessing; oh, let it rain, let … it … rain.

BRO. MIKE

(Rebuking.)

Yeah? Well … you are dangerously funny!

(Pauses.)

This is just too risky; possibly sinful too.

BRO. PAUL

Hey, bro! Don't cramp my style … come on!

BRO. MIKE

(Continues the scolding.)

I've been watching you look at them, week after week. This is just wrong. … You need to cease and desist. This type of behavior is totally unacceptable for a Christian … and especially on these premises.

BRO. PAUL

(Defensive.)

Well, don't blame *me*. To every action there is an equal and opposite reaction. I'm not the one you should be talking to.

(Pauses, pointing at the women.)

It's the offenders.

(Smiles again and starts to joke.)

*Shh!* Here comes another. I wonder, I wonder!

BRO. MIKE

(Seeming to join in.)

Why the grass is s-o-o-o-o green? And why you think it's okay for so much of them to be seen?

(Laughs.)

And who taught these ladies to dress?

Why do you ask? Because they need to put this type of fashion to rest?

(Smiles.)

Okay!

(Stops smiling.)

Let's get serious, because this is no laughing matter.

SIS. JESSIE

(Walks up to them; she wears a revealing outfit.)

Good morning.

BOTH

Good morning.

SIS. JESSIE

Beautiful morning, isn't it?

**"Do you see what I see?"**

BRO. PAUL
(Nods his head.)

It certainly is!

(Looks at her deviously.)

No need to ask how you are; can you take me with you?

SIS. JESSIE
(Smiling.)

I would, but we're already there.

BRO. PAUL
(Surprised.)

Where?

SIS. JESSIE

Here!

(A little annoyed, she holds up her Bible.)

Church!

BRO. PAUL
(Pretends to be naive.)

Silly me! I wonder why I thought you were going elsewhere.

BRO. MIKE
(Casts a sharp look at Bro. Paul.)

Probably because she forgot her jacket in the car!

SIS. JESSIE
(A little upset; uses a forceful tone.)

I did *not!* What's your problem?

BRO. MIKE
(Ignores her question.)

Ah … has anyone ever spoken to you about your mode of dress?

SIS. JESSIE
(Now obviously offended.)

What's wrong with the way I dress?

(Seething, she looks down at herself to double-check.)

There's no problem with my dress.

BRO. PAUL

Don't be so sure! Sister, there is a lot of room for improvement.

(Motioning to her appearance.)

Your look is just too … revealing.

(Starts to smile, shaking his head.)

Though, I have to admit, you are looking mighty fine.

BRO. MIKE

Hey, is that lust I see in your eyes?

BRO. PAUL

Probably!

(Defensive.)

Is there a problem?

BRO. MIKE

Well, quite possibly. Matthew 5:28 says, "But I say unto you, That whosoever looketh on a woman to lust after her hath committed adultery with her already in his heart."

SIS. JESSIE
(Playfully to Bro. Paul.)

Yeah … better be careful.

BRO. PAUL

Well, I'm human; I respond to what I see, hear, and feel. Moreover, to every *temptee,* there is a *tempter.* So, isn't that like the pot saying something bad about the kettle?

BRO. MIKE

(Turns to Sis. Jessie who appears displeased.)

It's true. You should know that wearing revealing clothes can stir up …

(Gesticulates with his hand.)

Um … lustful feelings in the heart of the person who is looking on. Like you just did to Brother Paul.

(Admonishes her.)

So, please be a little more thoughtful with your attire.

SIS. JESSIE

(Defensive.)

Well, don't blame me. When I came to church I saw how the other women dressed—and how they still dress—so … I thought it was okay.

BRO. PAUL

I understand, but how do you think your fellow church members really feel when you dress like this?

BRO. MIKE

More important, how does God feel? Is He pleased or disappointed?

SIS. JESSIE

Well, I know that He wants us all to look beautiful.

(Pauses, thinking.)

I know that beauty comes from within, but …

(Starts smiling.)

Trust me … some of us need a little prepping and painting on the outside too!

(Winks at them and then smiles broadly.)

…If you know what I mean.

BRO. MIKE

(Smiles.)

Oh, lady, I do. I honestly know what you're saying, but think about how you're offending God and everyone else. Things are just way out of hand.

SIS. JESSIE

(Teasing.)

Come on … a sister needs to be a little "in vogue" too.

BRO. PAUL

Trendy, eh? Well, nothing wrong with that. You just have to be choosy, so you don't break the rules. But, from what I can see here, you just want to totally blend in with those fashionistas, right?

SIS. JESSIE

Well, yeah! I don't want to look all plain and out of place.

BRO. MIKE

You mean you don't feel distinguished or special unless you are dressed like this?

SIS. JESSIE

Nope!

BRO. PAUL
(Cites 1 Peter 2:9.)

"But ye [are] a chosen generation, a royal priesthood, an holy nation, a peculiar people; that ye should shew forth the praises of him who hath called you out of darkness into his marvellous light."

BRO. MIKE

Right you are! The way that we dress is a silent but crucial declaration of our Christian principles.

BRO. PAUL

We need to dress differently, so that the very moment someone sees us they can say "There goes a Christian." I think you are a little too "hip" for us, Sister Jessie.

SIS. JESSIE
(Upset.)

Hey, don't make me your guinea pig or your whipping girl. I'm not the only one here like this.

BRO. MIKE

Sorry … we know, and that's why it's about time we say something about this.
(Pauses.)

As a matter of fact, it's long overdue.

BRO. PAUL

Point well taken, Sister; we understand. Don't let us keep you away from the service, now. See you later.

(She leaves; Bro. Carlton walks up and greets the other brothers.)

BRO. CARLTON

Hey bros, what's up?

BRO. MIKE

Sure you want to know?

BRO. CARLTON

Yeah! Why?

BRO. PAUL

Touchy subject!

BRO. CARLTON

Sure; go ahead.

BRO. MIKE

Okay, we were just talking about how some of our sisters dress, especially when coming to church.

BRO. PAUL
(Agrees.)

Yes! They need to realize that church is a place of worship, not a stage for a parade. I mean, sometimes nothing is left to the imagination.

BRO. CARLTON

Oh, come on! You know better than that. It's not our clothes that make us Christians; it is the lives that we live!

BRO. PAUL

Perhaps we live our lives through the clothes that we wear, though … right?

BRO. MIKE

That's right. We are not just what we wear; we become what we wear.

BRO. CARLTON

What do you mean?

BRO. MIKE

Have you ever noticed a woman in a revealing outfit? Tell me if she doesn't act that way—seductive … tempting.

BRO. PAUL

And the people with the expensive clothing, do they act God-centered?
No, they are very much self-centered, saying, "Over here … look at me; admire me … don't I look good?"

BRO. CARLTON

I get your point, but it's always such a pleasure to see them all dressed up … looking so nice and fine.

BRO. PAUL

Bro, be careful when you talk about looks. Remember Eve? She said the forbidden fruit was pleasing to the eye … now look at her descendants today —miserable!

BRO. MIKE

Look good? Yeah, right. We all need more self-control; more willpower to "just say no" to the seductive influence of fashion.

BRO. CARLTON

But the Bible does not give a typical way of dressing. Just accept it—things and times have changed.

BRO. PAUL

That's true, but Romans 12:2 says, "And be not conformed to this world: but be ye transformed by the renewing of your mind, that ye may prove what [is] that good, and acceptable, and perfect, will of God."

BRO. CARLTON
(Suddenly convinced.)

Wow! I see. … And you know what is so sad? Sometimes they dress a whole lot better to go to the office. Why? Because there is a dress code that is enforced.

BRO. MIKE

See what we're talking about? During the week, we go to work and show respect to our bosses, but then we come to church and disrespect God in our mode of dress.

BRO. PAUL

I know it's only getting worse; we have a responsibility to do something.

BRO. CARLTON

Yes, but what can we do?

BRO. MIKE

How about bringing it to the attention of the women's ministry?

BRO. PAUL

Good idea … but that's only for women. There may be other men who feel the same as we do, and they may want to express themselves.

BRO. CARLTON

Business meeting?

BRO. MIKE

Okay then! We'll try to get it on the agenda for the next meeting.
(Shakes Bro. Carl's hand.)

Thanks, bro, for coming on board.

BRO. CARLTON
(Sees someone coming.)

Wooh!

(Shakes his head, laughing.)

This one deserves a ticket.

BRO. MIKE
(Confused.)

A ticket? Are you insane?

BRO. CARLTON
(Pointing to the woman approaching.)

No, she is! Surely she deserves a ticket, because dressing like that, especially to come to church, is definitely against the law.

BRO. PAUL
(Having a change of heart, looks at the other two.)

Yeah, I know that there is no testimony without a test—but, come on! —the Lord does not want us to be tested like this … especially not at church.

BRO. MIKE
(Realizing who the woman is, looks at Bro. Carlton.)

Wow … look who is here!

BRO. CARLTON
(Surprised and embarrassed to see that it's his wife. Pronouncing it like *beautiful,* he croons.)

Cutie-ful! Darling … is that you?

SIS. ROSIE
(Proud and smiling.)

Your one and only!

BRO. CARLTON

What happened to the dress you had planned to wear?

SIS. ROSIE

Oh, that … I didn't like it. It made me look too plain. I decided to wear this one, instead … to surprise you.

BRO. CARLTON
(Sarcastic.)

Well, it worked … but … you shouldn't have.

BRO. PAUL
(Teasing Bro. Carlton.)

Wow! It's like *bam!* In your face.

BRO. MIKE
(Embarrassed for Bro. Carlton, and wanting to give him time alone with his wife; looks at his watch and beckons to Bro. Paul.)

Wooh … look at the time! Let's go. See you guys later.


(Bro. Paul and Bro. Carlton leave the stage.)

BRO. CARLTON
(Scolding his wife.)

What were you thinking? Can't you see that this is not appropriate for church? Or anywhere, for that matter.


SIS. ROSIE
(Complacent.)

That's not what my mirror told me.

(Trying to adjust her clothes, because they are so tight and the hem is so short.)

Although I was a whole lot more comfortable in the other one.

BRO. CARLTON

Yeah, the price of beauty! What's the sense of pulling and tugging on the dress to make it longer and more roomy, when you could have just bought your correct size in the first place?

SIS. ROSIE

Oh, come on, face it. … I look good, right?

BRO. CARLTON
(Mocking but stern.)

Oh, come on, face it! You need to go home and change your dress.

SIS. ROSIE
(Calmly, as she continues to adjust her clothes.)

No, darling … no … can … do. I won't have enough time; I have to sing the song of meditation.

BRO. CARLTON
(Stunned.)

*What?!* Dressed like that? Do you realize that people will actually see you?

**SIS. ROSIE**

Well, duh! That's the idea … to be seen! So I have to look my best.

**BRO. CARLTON**

Or your worst. Isn't it almost sacrilegious to do that? What disrespect for God and His sanctuary … and your fellow believers.

**SIS. ROSIE**

(Unconcerned.)

Look at you. Why are you freaking out like that?

**BRO. CARLTON**

(Holds up his hands, exasperated.)

Satan, Satan, why are you are testing me like this?

**SIS. ROSIE**

(Upset.)

Have you lost your mind? … Don't call me that!

**BRO. CARLTON**

(Without compassion.)

Well, I wasn't, but … if the cap fits. …

**SIS. ROSIE**

Hey, what's gotten into you? You used to love it when I dressed like this.

**BRO. CARLTON**

Yes, that's true. But … now I am using my 20/20 vision.

(Pulls up his pants at the waist to show that he is taking charge.)

Things are going to change … big time. It's about time I start to exercise some control over my household.

**SIS. ROSIE**

(With a rebellious attitude.)

Oh, I see where this is leading. So now you're going to start telling me how to dress, eh?

BRO. CARLTON

(Calmly.)

Oh no, honey. I wouldn't do that. ... I would like to have some peace.

SIS. ROSIE

(Smiles.)

Oh, how smart.

BRO. CARLTON

But, you can be at war with God ... because He already does.

SIS. ROSIE

(Upset.)

What? ... Cheap shot.

BRO. CARLTON

Really? How cheap is this? Matthew 16:24 says, "...If any man would come after me, let him deny himself and take up his cross and follow me." Well, does it seem like you have denied anything ... or are you bearing any cross, dressed like that?

SIS. ROSIE

But, I'm singing. Isn't that taking up the cross? Doesn't that count for something?

BRO. CARLTON

That's even worse. How can we witness and expect to win over the world, if we cannot even choose to look different?

SIS. ROSIE

But my witnessing is with my singing.

BRO. CARLTON

No, your witnessing is not just limited to your singing; it involves everything about you. Moreover, people see you before they hear you ... right?

SIS. ROSIE

(Unsure.)

Well, yeah. ...

BRO. CARLTON

So how ironic that those who really want to be witnessed to … by you … with your singing … may have to actually close their eyes when they see you, although your intention is to be seen.

SIS. ROSIE

(Lightbulb moment; she sobers.)

What … my clothes are a distraction?

BRO. CARLTON

(Lifts his hand.)

Thank you, Jesus—the lights got turned on.

SIS. ROSIE

Are you saying that they'll pay more attention to my clothes than to the song?

BRO. CARLTON

(Happy and smiling.)

Keep the light shining; don't let Satan blow it out. Let it shine … let it shine. … Let … it … shine!

SIS.ROSIE

(Reflective.)

Wow, amazing! Dressing simply is one of the ways for us Christians to let our light shine. I never thought about it like that before. But … it is true. … As Christians we are held to a much higher standard in everything.

BRO. CARLTON

(Still smiling; teases her.)

That's why you're my wife. So perceptive!

SIS. ROSIE

(Pacing and thinking.)

And as a person participating in the worship sessions, my standards should be set even higher, because to whom much is given, much is expected. … I have to first do, and then ask them to do likewise.

BRO. CARLTON

(Jumps up, excited.)

Hallelujah! You got it!

SIS. ROSIE

Well, no more disrespecting my God … and you all.

(Points to her husband.)

I am ready to change my way of dress, because I want to show everyone who I really am.

(Thinking.)

Wow … now I'm going to have to find someone to give these clothes to.


BRO. CARLTON

Oh no! What is not good for the goose is not good for the gander. You cannot encourage other people to dress like this when you are not.


SIS. ROSIE

(Smiles.)

Sorry … wasn't thinking. Well …

(Clears her throat.)

Darling, get out the debit card, 'cause we're going shopping! It's time for a new wardrobe.


BRO. CARLTON

(Puts hand over his pocket, looking surprised, because he had not thought about the cost of new clothes.)

Aaahhh!

# SCENE II

(A business meeting is in progress.)

## BRO. BARRY

The next item on the agenda is "Altar Fashion."
(Surprised.)
What? Very interesting. Who knows what this is about?

## BRO. MIKE

Well, there is a serious decline in the way we clothe ourselves as Christians, in general, but especially when coming into the house of the Lord.

## BRO. PAUL

We have an identity crisis where Christian fashion is concerned. … I'm pretty sure that the way some of us dress, most of the time, is not in the least pleasing to our God.

## SIS. NANCY

(Defensive.)
Excuse me? My God is not superficial. … He says to come as you are.

## BRO. CARLTON

You're so right. But we are not to stay as we are. As Christians we ought to be growing each day. When we have been transformed, we should be wearing a look that says, "See how The Lord has changed me from the inside out."

## BRO. BARRY

Yep, we need to be more easily identified.

## SIS. JESSIE

(Sarcastic.)
What would you like … for us to dress in uniforms like the postman and the police officer?

### BRO. MIKE

Not a bad idea; at least we know who they are.

(Chuckles.)

You see, if you want to be taken seriously as a Christian, you cannot be masquerading in the devil's outfit.


### SIS. NANCY

Hello! Their clothes might not be perfect, but their hearts are in the right place—unlike some of you.


### SIS. MONICA

(In a preachy manner.)

See … it's nice that Jesus has our hearts, but that's just a part of us. Correct me if I am wrong, but doesn't he want all of us? As far as I am aware, it is all or nothing.


### BRO. MIKE

Moreover, Matthew 12:34 says, "….Out of the abundance of the heart the mouth speaketh." So, there you go, you first have to think that way in your heart before you decide to dress in that manner.


### BRO. CARLTON

Oh boy! Next thing we'll hear is that it doesn't matter, because that's not what is taking us to heaven … we are saved by grace.


### SIS. JESSIE

Well, yeah! We *are* saved by grace, and grace only—God's gift to us.


### BRO. PAUL

Sure, we all are, but when we accept Jesus' grace and become saved …

(Shakes his head.)

Oh, what a transformation! We become like new creatures—talking, acting, and looking different.


### BRO. MIKE

Romans 12:1 says, "I beseech you therefore, brethren, by the mercies of God, that ye present your bodies a living sacrifice, holy, acceptable unto God, [which is] your reasonable service."

SIS. ROSIE

And remember the second verse: "And be not conformed to this world: but be ye transformed by the renewing of your mind, that ye may prove what [is] that good, and acceptable, and perfect, will of God."

SIS. MONICA

Yes, the inner rebirth is reflected in the outward appearance, so you all need to stop shopping at those "See-More" stores.

SIS. JESSIE

What?

(To Sis. Nancy.)

What store is that?

SIS. NANCY

Never heard of it.

SIS. MONICA

Really? That's funny. Well, you wear their brand all the time, because we are always seeing more of you—and less of the clothes.

BRO. BARRY

There is a time and place for everything, but when we are Christians we have to ensure that we wear our uniform at all times.

SIS. NANCY
(Confused and upset.)

*Aaahhh?!*

BRO. PAUL
(Clarifying.)

We have to wear the Christian uniform, called "modesty."

BRO. MIKE

Dressing modestly means to dress in a way that is considered proper and decent. It also means having a quiet and humble appearance.

SIS. MONICA

This not only shows respect for ourselves, but for others—and ... most important ... for God.

SIS. JESSIE
(Rebuking.)

Humble, eh? What about all you men who buy these real expensive suits, instead of taking care of your homes? Isn't there a problem with that?

SIS. ROSIE

Oh yes!

SIS. NANCY

And then there are those who think it is fashionable to wear those sagging pants—showing the make, model, and all of their undergarments.

SIS. ROSIE

As if we are interested! And then they are surprised when they are mistaken for a criminal.

BRO. MIKE

Wooh!

SIS. MONICA

And what about those who dress so modestly to come to church, but then at other places not even their own family members can recognize them … unless they greet them first, of course.

SIS. ROSIE
(Taps her jaw with her finger.)

Wow! These are questions that make you go *mmmm*.

BRO. PAUL

That's despicable. Whether men or women, we have to be very careful of the message we send by the way we dress … at all times.

BRO. CARLTON

Yes. Did you know that our physical presentation, which includes the way we dress, is possibly the most important nonverbal communicator of our moral values?

SIS. JESSIE
(Still resisting.)

You need to try to work with us instead of judging us. …
(Points her finger at the group.)

Never judge a book by its cover.

BRO. PAUL

So true, Sister! We live up to that quite well, don't we? 'Cause looking at some of us, one certainly could never tell that we are Christians.

SIS. JESSIE
(Frustrated; waves her hand at him.)

Whatever!

SIS. MONICA

Oh yeah? That's what you'd like us to believe, but my God is not a "whatever" God.
(Imitates Sis. Jessie's hand movement.)
He has standards, and so should we.

SIS. NANCY

So what? It's true that Christians are held to a higher standard, but you can't legislate how people should dress … that's just ridiculous.

SIS. ROSIE

Oh, girl, I know how you feel.

SIS. NANCY
(Grateful.)

See? … Thank you. Come on, tell them.

SIS. ROSIE

You know the truth, but you just want to have your cake and eat it too!

SIS. NANCY
(Surprised and upset.)

What? You … you set me up! So typical of you … "gotcha" Christians.

SIS. ROSIE
(Smirks.)

Well, I said I knew how you feel … I didn't say that I agreed.

SIS. JESSIE

(Thinking.)

Okay, I think I finally got it. The clothes are our picture frames, and we are the actual pictures. … People see us before they get a chance to talk to us, to find out that we are Christians, so we have to be very careful.

SIS. NANCY

(Lightbulb moment; covers her mouth with her hand, opens eyes wide, and then moves hand away, exclaiming.)

Wow! Maybe that's why some people act so surprised when I say that I am a Christian.

BRO. CARLTON

There you go!

SIS. NANCY

Oh my goodness, what was I thinking? We are what we eat; we are what we say; so of course we are what we wear! Duh!

SIS. ROSIE

(Regretful.)

I know as Christians it is our responsibility to draw others closer to Christ, not to turn them away. I hope the Lord will forgive me for all the people I have offended.

SIS. MONICA

(Sympathetic.)

I'm sure He will. See, in your ignorance, The Lord winks at you, but James 4:17says, "Therefore to him that knoweth to do good, and doeth it not, to him it is a sin."

BRO. MIKE

Yes, we should always be mindful of the fact that we have the power to create a permanent influence on others by what we wear. What we look like reflects on the Lord.

BRO. PAUL

If we do not know who we are, we could be living like someone else. God has given us dress guidelines as part our identity; let's use them.

BRO. BARRY
(Clears his throat.)

Finally, brethren, if your outfit is not legit—or your look is not according to the book—think on these things.

BRO. MIKE

These things that you have heard today, do them, because you are being profiled by the Holy One, to weed out those who have been defiled.

SIS. JESSIE
(Cites 1 Cor. 6:19.)

Remember, "your body is the temple of the Holy Ghost .......and ye are not your own"...... So don't desecrate it.

SIS. NANCY

And cover it up properly, 'cause …

SIS. ROSIE

It's all good! …

BRO. CARLTON

And … it's a beautiful thing!

**THE END**

# 3

# Your "Neighbortunity"

## Service Is the Christian's Duty

"And, behold, a certain lawyer stood up, and tempted him, saying, Master, what shall I do to inherit eternal life?.......

And he answering said, Thou shalt love the Lord thy God with all thy heart, and with all thy soul, and with all thy strength, and with all thy mind; and thy neighbour as thyself......

But he, willing to justify himself, said unto Jesus, And who is my neighbour?"
(Luke 10:25–29)

We were placed here to care for each other. However, our lives have become so busy that we have forgotten some very important principles, such as seeking opportunities to assist those in need. This play is about service, and it is a modern-day interpretation of the parable of the good Samaritan.

# CHARACTERS

VICTIM  Injured car driver; torn clothes, bruised and battered body.

PASTOR  Uncaring and arrogant; dressed in an expensive suit; drives a luxury car.

ELDER  Self-absorbed; priorities are all mixed up. More concerned with doing church work than with helping others. Could be a male or female. (Wears a church hat and very modest clothing, if female; wears a suit if male.)

RASTA-MAN  Businessman; humble and thoughtful. Well dressed, in Rastafarian clothing. The colors red, green, yellow, and black are quite prominent in his attire. Has a strong Jamaican accent.

NURSE  Christian; very compassionate. Dresses in a nurse's scrub uniform; has a stethoscope around her neck.

# SETTING

Victim is in the road on Alligator Alley, Florida (a very lonely stretch of road). He was on his way from Miami to Naples, when he was robbed and beaten. They just left him to die.

Victim was later taken to a Christian hospital for treatment.

# TIME

Late afternoon. And three days later.

# SCENE I

(Victim is partially in the road. He is bloody and almost immobile; clothes are torn. Canals are on either sides of road. There is fence on both sides, with alligators quite visible.)

## VICTIM
(Trying to move; clearly in pain.)

*Ooh! … aah!* I better try to get out of the road before someone runs over me.
> (He is unable to do so, for he is too weak and battered. He hears the sound of a car horn blowing.)

## PASTOR

*Beep, beep, beep!*

> (Vehicle stops, and someone steps out.)

## VICTIM
(Glances up, seeing someone he recognizes.)

Oh, thank You, God! You sent me an angel. Thank You, thank You!

## PASTOR
(Looks at victim, looks at himself, and then looks at victim again; clearly disgusted.)

So much blood and dirt!!

> (Frustrated; paces back and forth.)

Ah … no … no. My suit is too expensive; it will just get ruined. Chances are, I'll never get blood stains out of this.

> (Looks around to see if anyone sees him; shrugs.)

Well, you win some and you lose some. … Sorry, son, not today.

> (Gets back into his car and drives around Victim.)

## VICTIM
(Gasps.)

Father, did you hear that? And, could you just f-e-e-e-el the love, because I certainly could not.

> (Takes a deep breath.)

"Love is patient; love is kind … love is patient; love is kind … love is patient; love is kind. Father, please help me to believe that."

ELDER

*Beep, beep, beep.*


VICTIM

Good—here comes someone else. Help! Help!


ELDER
                    (Stops the car, gets out, and sadly looks at Victim.)
Wooh! This one looks like he needs an ambulance.
                    (Looks at watch to check time; now visibly irritated.)
But … I can't wait for any ambulance now! Moreover, he doesn't even seem like he is going to make it.
                    (Looks up and prays.)
O Lord, you know my heart. You know that I am a good person, but I … I wouldn't want to keep the others at prayer meeting waiting for me.
                    (Pauses.)
You know how I hate to be late.
                    (Starts to walk away, but then looks around at Victim.)
I'll pray for you—and your soul, if necessary.
                    (Gets back into the car, leaving Victim lying in the road.)


VICTIM
                    (Very disappointed.)
Satan is a liar; I can't believe he just left me like this!
                    (Pauses.)
You're right; God knows your heart … I'll pray for you too!
                    (Still waiting for help, starts to pray.)
Father … You told me that You will never leave me nor forsake me. I know You won't, so please send me someone soon. … Anyone.


RASTA-MAN
                    (From a distance sees something in the road.)
Oh, these animals are always crossing the street, but this one was not so fortunate. Looks like another one bites the dust!

VICTIM
(Opens eyes and sees Rasta-Man before he gets out of
his car.)

O Lord, please!

(He rethinks.)

Okay, Lord—I'll have to trust you on this one too.

RASTA-MAN
(Gets closer.)

Uh-oh, it's not an animal … it's a man!

(Gets out of the car and tries to talk to Victim. He bends
close to Victim's ear, shouting.)

Hey, mon! Ya dead?

VICTIM
(Pretends to be dead; gives no response.)

RASTA-MAN
(Bends down and feels for a pulse by the wrist and neck;
smiles; lifts up his hands toward heaven.)

Thank you, Jah! He's alive!

(Speaks in a loud voice again, bending over Victim.)

Hey, mon, ya hearing me?

VICTIM
(Nervous; answers in a soft voice.)

Yes.

RASTA-MAN

Okay, just hang on, mon. I'm gonna to try to get help for you. Okay?

VICTIM

Okay.

**"He needs an ambulance, but I can't be late for prayer meeting"**

RASTA-MAN
(Walking back to his car for a blanket, he looks at his watch, stops, and contemplates.)

Oh no! I'm going to be late for my meeting with the producer.
(Pauses, thinking.)

But ... well ...
(Paces back and forth, still thinking and trying to decide what to do.)

I certainly would not like anyone to ignore me, leave me lying in the road like this.
(Cites Luke 6:31.)

The Golden Rule does say, "Do unto others as you would like them to do to you."


VICTIM
(Overhearing.)

You're going to be late? I'm sorry to be so much trouble!


RASTA-MAN
(Apologetic.)

Oh no ... no trouble at all.
(Comes back with blanket, bends to put it under Victim's head, and then stands up; reflecting on Matthew 16:26.)

Yeah, money is important, but in the grave this soul will be priceless!


VICTIM
(Cites Luke 12:34.)

Well, it is quite obvious where your heart and treasure is.


RASTA-MAN
(Cites Romans 12:10.)

Mon, this is the way I see it: We should "Be kindly affectioned one to another with brotherly love; in honour preferring one another." So, tell me, what happened?


VICTIM

I tried to help someone but, instead, I was robbed and beaten, as you can see.

RASTA-MAN

Sorry to hear that; hang in there, mon—you'll be fine.

> (Pulls out his phone from his Rasta hat and tries to call 911, but the call does not go through. He looks at the phone.)

Oh no! I have no bars; no reception.

> (Moves around, but cannot get a signal.)

VICTIM

None?

RASTA-MAN

None!

> (Looks at Victim, thinking.)

Hey, you have a cell phone, mon? Maybe your service is better than mine.

VICTIM

No, they took it and all my money … everything!

RASTA-MAN

I'm really sorry to hear that. … Well, looks like I'll have to turn around to take you to the hospital, mon.

> (Thinking out loud.)

There goes my meeting, but … no problem, mon; when one door is closed many more are opened.

> (Picks up Victim, puts him in the car, gets in, and heads him to the hospital.)

# SCENE II

(At the hospital, Rasta-Man stops at the nurses' station.)

RASTA-MAN

Nursie, how are you today?

NURSE

(Looks up from her clipboard; she smiles, recognizing him.)

Great!

RASTA-MAN

And the patient?

NURSE

(Still smiling.)

Wonderful, Mr. Hero!

RASTA-MAN

(Humble.)

Who? Me? I just did what anyone else would have done.

NURSE

Are you kidding me? You have no idea! Two other persons just passed him by, left him for dead.

RASTA-MAN

(Surprised.)

Oh no! That's just mean.

(Shakes his head.)

Cold … ice-cold hearts.

NURSE

(Almost whispering.)

He mentioned a Pastor and an Elder, can you imagine?

RASTA-MAN
(Looks up, holding up his hand.)

Mercy!

NURSE
(Sad; lowers eyes.)

That's an irony, because they are supposed to have the warmest hearts.

(Perks up, looking at him; cites Matthew 5:14– 16.)

Anyways, when you are the light of the world, you have to let your light shine before us all, that your good works be seen.

(Puts up both hands.)

To God be the glory.

RASTA-MAN
(Quite humble.)

Well, thank you. That's how it should be.

NURSE
(Still praising him.)

He just cannot stop talking about the nice stranger—you, of course—who helped him. He thinks you actually saved his life.

RASTA-MAN
(Pleased.)

I probably did, but I consider it my duty to help when I can, and especially with strangers. My grandma always tells me, "Be kind to everyone, especially to strangers." Don't know why, but I've always done that; just seems like the right thing to do.

NURSE
(Enlightens him.)

I know. Hebrews 13:2 says, "Be not forgetful to entertain strangers: for thereby some have entertained angels unawares." So your grandma taught you well.

RASTA-MAN
(Thoughtful, and then excited; wondering if the patient was actually an angel.)

Really? That's very interesting! But he was for real, right?

NURSE

(Smiling.)

Yes, he's a real person. However, sometimes God sends an angel to test a person's character, and we do not ever want to fail that test.


RASTA-MAN

(Thinking.)

*Hmmm!* But, Nursie, the others before me did fail, if the person I helped was supposed to be an angel, right?


NURSE

Exactly!

(Cites 1 John 4:20.)

"…For he that loveth not his brother whom he hath seen, how can he love God whom he hath not seen?" God wants us to be kind, loving and merciful at all times—to everyone—'cause … you never know.

(Looks at him.)

There is no doubt in my mind that you know what love is.


RASTA-MAN

Well, you know sometimes we're so preoccupied with our concerns, and that gets in the way of helping others.

(Shakes his head.)

Such a shame!


NURSE

Yes, but we have to be very careful.

(Cites 1 John 4:7.)

God says "Beloved, let us love one another: for love is of God; and every one that loveth is born of God, and knoweth God." I think that refers to you.


RASTA-MAN

Thanks; I was just doing my brotherly duties. Anyway, what about the bill?


NURSE

Oh, it's good. He has health insurance.

RASTA-MAN
(Looks relieved; laughs.)
Great, 'cause I don't have any money, but … Jah will always provide.
(Turns his head to look around.)
Where is he, anyway?


NURSE
Room 331, down the hall, on the right; follow me.

# SCENE III

(At Victim's bedside; Nurse walks into room, followed by Rasta-Man [Good Samaritan].)

NURSE
(To Victim.)

Well, look who's here to see you!

RASTA-MAN
(Greets Victim.)

Hey, mon!! You're looking great today.

NURSE
(Goes back to nurses' station to fill out some paperwork.)

VICTIM

Yes, my neighbor ... I'm feeling just wonderful

RASTA-MAN
(Surprised; smiles.)

Neighbor? Look at that! Good thing I had stopped to help you, because I had no idea that we lived close to each other.

VICTIM

Oh, we don't. The Bible says that anyone in need of your help is your neighbor.

RASTA-MAN

Oh ... now I see. ... You needed my help, so ...

VICTIM

(Almost crying.)

Yes, and indeed you are a good neighbor.

(Cites Matthew 25:35–39.)

"For I was an hungred, and ye gave me meat: I was thirsty, and ye gave me drink: I was a stranger, and ye took me in. Naked, and ye clothed me: I was sick, and ye visited me: I was in prison, and ye came unto me."

(Now crying openly.)

(Nurse returns to Victim's bedside.)

RASTA-MAN

(Consoling him.)

Okay, don't get all mushy on me now!

NURSE

(Interjects, citing Matthew 25:40.)

One day the Lord will say to you, "Verily I say unto you, Inasmuch as ye have done [it] unto one of the least of these my brethren, ye have done [it] unto me."

RASTA-MAN

(Cites 1 John 2:15.)

"Love not the world, neither the things [that are] in the world."

(Pauses and chuckles)

But, love the people in the world, right?

NURSE

(Nods her head.)

Right!

(Turns to Victim.)

Now, as for those that left you behind, they really messed up, and they'll be very sorry.

VICTIM

(Regains his composure.)

Oh yes! They'll be knocking on the gate, saying, "Jesus, you forgot us, let us in."

NURSE

And Jesus will say, "Excuse me, but who are you?"

VICTIM

And they'll say, "Come on, Jesus, don't you remember us? We used to preach, and sing, and spread your words and win souls for you."

NURSE

(Continues what Victim started.)

"And we use to hold prayer vigils and give out tracks."

RASTA-MAN

But that's all good, right?

VICTIM

Well, yeah, to a point. ... But Jesus will say, "What about when I was hungry and thirsty and sick and naked and in prison? Where were you? What did you do?

NURSE

(Reaches over to reposition the oxygen in Victim's nostrils.)

Then they'll say, "Jesus, when were you ever in such a need that we did not jump right in, with both feet, and help?" Come on Lord, this is not a time for kidding; it's really hot out here. ... It feels like hell!

RASTA-MAN

But it is!

VICTIM

That's right! Then Jesus will say, "Do you remember the old man who came to your house begging for food, but you ignored him, because he looked like he did not belong to the neighborhood?"

NURSE

When they have no answer, Jesus will say, "And the person with the broken-down car next to your business. You thought he was a nuisance, so you chased him away when you could have helped him. He was bad for your business, remember?"

RASTA-MAN

And they'll say what? "Oh snap! ... Jesus, was that you? Why, why didn't you say so?"

**NURSE**

And Jesus will say, "Oh yes, that was I. The homeless, the street beggar, the sick, the naked, the destitute ... your neighbor!"

**VICTIM**

Then they'll say, "Okay, Jesus, we're so sorry; it won't happen again."
(Begging and fanning himself.)
"Please let us in, Jesus; we really need some air conditioning."

**NURSE**

But, Jesus will say, "Uh-uh. Don't want to hear it!"

**RASTA-MAN**

I know, He'll say, "Too late ... talk ... to ... the gate!"

**NURSE**

(Cites Matthew 25:45.)
Yes, the King will reply, "Verily I say unto you, Inasmuch as ye did [it] not to one of the least of these, ye did [it] not to me."

**VICTIM**

(Takes a deep breath and turns to Rasta-Man.)
I'm so grateful to you for saving my life. Sometimes the people we expect help from disappoint us; but on the other hand, the people we expect the least from are the ones who bring us real joy.

**RASTA-MAN**

(To the audience/congregation.)
Well, if we'd all just put a little love in our hearts, this world would be a much better place.

**VICTIM**

(To Rasta-Man.)
You're so right.

(Turns head to glances at the audience/congregation.)
Just do your brotherly and sisterly duties.

**NURSE**

(To audience/congregation.)
Yes! Want to inherit eternal life? Be a good neighbor!

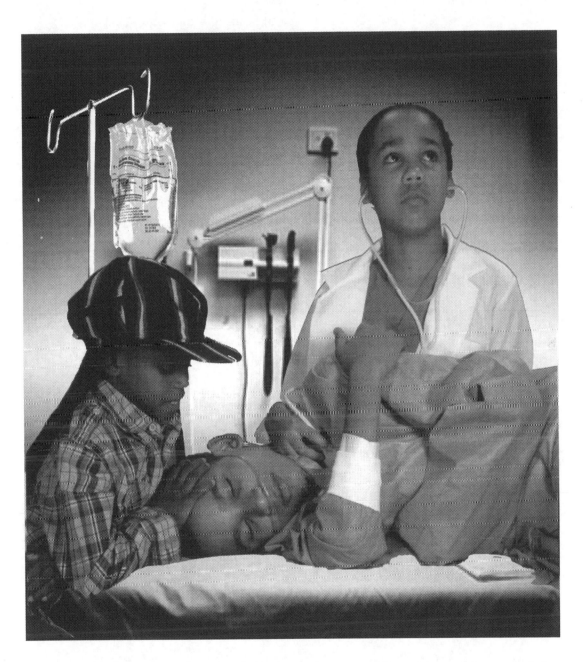

**'If we'd all just put a little love in our hearts, this world would be a much better place"**

RASTA-MAN

Go and do likewise, and you'll get some cool breeze.

(Smiling and fanning himself.)

ALL

(Chuckle and give the thumbs-up.)

No problem, mon!

**THE END**

# 4

# To Die For

## Obedience Is the Main Ingredient in Worship

"And the LORD God caused a deep sleep to fall upon Adam, and he slept: and he took one of his ribs…..And the rib, which the LORD God had taken from man, made he a woman, and brought her unto the man." (Genesis. 2:21, 22)

"Now the serpent was more subtil than any beast of the field which the LORD God had made. And he said unto the woman, Yea, hath God said, Ye shall not eat of every tree of the garden?" (Genesis 3:1).

And the LORD God said unto the serpent, Because thou hast done this, thou art cursed …….upon thy belly shalt thou go, and dust shalt thou eat all the days of thy life: (Genesis 3:14).

"Unto the woman he said, I will greatly multiply thy sorrow and thy conception; in sorrow thou shalt bring forth children; and thy desire [shall be] to thy husband, and he shall rule over thee." (Genesis 3:16)

Then to Adam He said: "Because thou hast hearkened unto the voice of thy wife, …. cursed [is] the ground for thy sake; in sorrow shalt thou eat [of] it all the days of thy life………In the sweat of thy face shalt thou eat bread, till thou return unto the ground; for out of it wast thou taken: for dust thou [art], and unto dust shalt thou return." (Genesis 3:17,19.)

And the LORD God said, Behold, the man is become as one of us, to know good and evil: and now, lest he put forth his hand, and take also of the tree of life, and eat, and live for ever. Therefore the LORD God sent him forth from the garden of Eden." (Genesis 3:22,23).

We were created by God, but He gave us freedom of choice. There are consequences for all our actions, whether good or bad. This play is about obedience, recognizing temptation, and living with the consequences of giving in to it.

# CHARACTERS

ADAM — Handsome young man, dressed in white gown; (Gown closes with Velcro for easy removal. A skin-tone body suit is to be worn below and exposed when he realizes that he is naked. Have large leaves available to be placed in the appropriate spots when he returns onstage.)

EVE — Beautiful young woman; same mode of dress as Adam.

SERPENT — Prop in tree; actor offstage throughout play; must have a seductive, convincing voice.

GOD — Hidden; actor offstage throughout play; must have an authoritative voice.

ANGELS — Optional, depending on how many people are available, and also the timing desired for the play.

ANGEL OF DEATH

# SETTING

Story takes place in the garden of Eden; lots of trees, flowers, and animals. A snake should be visible in the tree when Eve is talking to him.

Also takes place outside of the garden, where the environment is unattractive, uninviting, and depressing—no greenery, no flowers, and no (pleasant) animals.

If possible, split the stage from scene II onward, as there will be frequent changes between scenes.

# TIME

Shortly before and after Adam and Eve sin.

# SCENE I

(Adam lies sleeping. He wakes up, surprised to find Eve looking at him.)

ADAM

(Yawns and stretches, leans his neck to the left and then to the right, puts his hands together, and stretches again.)

Wow, that was such a good sleep.

(Looks around, notices Eve, and then looks up, surprised.)

Wooh! Where did such a beauty come from?

EVE

(Moves away a little, laughs, and points at Adam.)

From *you*.

ADAM

(Points to himself, puzzled.)

*Me?* How? ...

(He gets up and starts to examine Eve—her hair, her skin; anything that looks different from him.)

EVE

(Explaining.)

God put you into a deep sleep, and then He took one of your ribs to make me from a part of you.

ADAM

(Adam peeks under his gown, looking at the skin of his rib area; Eve notices.)

EVE

Yeah, you're already healed.

ADAM
(Holds Eve by her shoulders; slowly slides his hands down her arms.)
You are bones of my bones and flesh of my flesh.
(Smiles, looks away, and then acts as if he just won a prize, throwing up his hands joyfully.)
Hallelujah! My prayers have been answered.
(Turns back toward Eve, smiling broadly.)
You know, we'll have a permanent connection.

EVE
(Giggles.)
Funny!

ADAM
(Moves closer to Eve, gazing at her invitingly.)
May I?

EVE
(Nods approvingly.)

ADAM
(Touches Eve's skin and hair.)
All things bright and beautiful, the Lord God made them all.

EVE
(Smiles.)

ADAM
(Still captivated by Eve's presence.)
Amazing! Since you are a part of me, you will be called "wo-man".

EVE
(Beams with delight.)

ADAM
And you are the mother of all living, so you will be called "Eve".

EVE

Oh, that sounds just wonderful!


ADAM
(Reflective; starts walking. Eve follows.)
I actually thought the garden was so beautiful, just as it was, but—
(Turns to look at Eve.)
With you here, now it is perfect; you complete me.
(Takes her hand.)
Come, let me show you around.


(They walk around the garden. Adam points at different things, while Eve looks on in amazement. He finds a flower, picks it, and puts it in her hair. He stops by the Tree of Life, looking very pleased. He continues to the Tree of Knowledge of Good and Evil, and there he stops, warning Eve to keep away from that tree.)

# SCENE II

(Adam works in the garden, enjoying his chores of grooming the animals and caring for the plants. Eve wanders away, but Adam does not notice. She senses that she is not alone, and becomes afraid momentarily; she pauses, about to return to Adam, but then she just shrugs, continuing on her way. Eve passes the Tree of Life. She looks around, admiring the trees, plants, birds, insects, and animals that fill the garden. Stopping at the Tree of Knowledge of Good and Evil, she stares at it with some doubt, turning her head to the left and then to the right. She puts her fingers to her lips, tapping them as if she is thinking.)

SERPENT
(Prop in tree; voice offstage throughout play.)

*Psst!*

EVE
(Looks around for a few seconds, but sees nothing; resumes thinking.)

SERPENT

*Psst!* Over here.

EVE
(Notices Serpent in the tree; stares at him for a few seconds before speaking.)

Was that you just calling me?

SERPENT
(A bit impatient.)

Well, yeah!

EVE
(Still stunned.)

Wooh! A talking serpent? That's just way too cool.

SERPENT
(Very seductively.)

You like?

(OPTIONAL: Two Angels fly in to protect Eve; they are on either side of her; both wear signs that say, "Heaven's Secret Service".)

EVE
(Still in awe. Addresses Serpent.)

Of course! Wow, you're so adorable.

FIRST ANGEL

No, Eve, he's not; he only appears to be.

EVE
(Puzzled; turns to see who just spoke, but Serpent interjects.)

SERPENT

Know where I got the powers to do that?

EVE
(Excited; and moves a little closer to tree.)

SECOND ANGEL

He can hurt you, Eve. … I'm telling you, he's not as nice as he seems.

EVE
(Ignores Angel; turns toward Serpent, captivated.)

Where?

SECOND ANGEL
(Throws up his hands in the air, as if to say "unbelievable!".)

SERPENT

This tree.

EVE
(Surprised.)

This tree? No way!


SERPENT

Uh-huh!


EVE

Yeah? How?


SERPENT

I ate this juicy fruit.


EVE
(Intrigued; starts to admire the tree again.)

Really?!

# SCENE III

(Adam seems happy; still singing and working. Scene should last approximately thirty seconds.)

# SCENE IV

#### SECOND ANGEL
(Tries to hurry Eve along.)
Come on, Eve, move it, move it; time to go.

#### FIRST ANGEL
(Agrees.)
Don't idle, Eve, especially here. … This could be a real disaster!

#### SERPENT
Well, it's a total waste to just admire it, Eve! Come on, have one.

#### EVE
(Moves to pick the fruit.)

#### SERPENT
(Sounds very happy.)
Good, girl!

#### FIRST ANGEL
(Shocked; shouting.)
No-o-o-o-o, Eve! Don't do it!

#### SECOND ANGEL
(Pleading.)
Listen, not all that glitters is gold!

# SCENE V

(Third Angel appears to Adam, who is still in the garden, singing and working.)

THIRD ANGEL

Hey, Adam. … Adam … ADAM!

ADAM

(Stops working; looks around, confused.)

THIRD ANGEL

Stop what you're doing right now, Adam! Go find your wife; she is about to get into some serious trouble. … Hurry!

ADAM

(Suddenly realizes that Eve is missing. Looks for her in one direction, but doesn't see her. He turns his head in the other direction, but there is still no sign of her. He starts to call for her.)

Eve? … Eve? … Where are you?

THIRD ANGEL

(With a sense of urgency.)

She is on the other side of the garden; she will not hear you like this. Go!

ADAM

(Turns to go; stops, hesitating.)

Ah … I'm sure she's just fine.

THIRD ANGEL

(Shakes his head.)

No, Adam, she's not fine! Oh … you have no idea what's going down.

ADAM

(Continues to work happily.)

# SCENE VI

(On the other side of the garden Eve suddenly remembers what she was told about the tree; she withdraws her hand. Throughout scene Angels address Eve, but she ignores them, paying attention only to the Serpent; Eve only addresses Serpent.)

EVE

Oh no! I can't.

FIRST ANGEL
(Relieved.)

Whew! Wow, Eve! For a moment I actually thought you were going to do it. You finally came to your senses. Okay, now, run along before it's too late.

SECOND ANGEL

Believe me, he is very smart, Eve. Extremely slick too; don't hang around!

SERPENT
(Pretends to be surprised.)

Why not, Eve? "You may not eat of every tree?"

EVE
(Unsure of herself.)

No.

SERPENT
(Sarcastic.)

Bummer! Oh, I know, all fruits are created equal, but some are more equal than others, right?

EVE

Well, I wouldn't say that. God told Adam and I that we can eat of every tree—

SERPENT
(Interrupts.)

Except this one.

(In a mocking tone.)

He is so generous, but He is placing restrictions on you.

FIRST ANGEL
(To Second Angel.)

Why doesn't she listen to us?

SECOND ANGEL

She is throwing away her whole future for a worthless piece of fruit.

EVE

Well, God says we should not even touch it.

SERPENT
(Taunting.)

Wow! Well, I have to tell you, Eve, you are really missing out.

EVE
(Concerned.)

I am?

SERPENT

Sure.

FIRST ANGEL

No, you're not, Eve! Whatever you're missing out on is nothing good.

SECOND ANGEL

Trust me, Eve—the Lord will not withhold anything that's good from you.

EVE
(Confused; questions Serpent.)

How so? This is the Tree of Knowledge of Good and Evil, right?

SERPENT

Right! ... And that's why He does not want you to eat of it, because you'll gain too much knowledge.

EVE

Oh no. That's not what He said. God said that the day that we eat of it we will surely die.

SERPENT
(Laughs.)

Ha, ha, ha, ha, *h-a-a-a!* Die? Oh no! Instead, you'll become as wise as He is, and He does not want that to happen.

EVE
(Excited.)

Really? I'll become wiser? And be ... ?

SERPENT

Anything ... even a god.

(Eve fantasizes about her future power.)

FIRST ANGEL
(Still pleading.)

Listen to me, Eve, don't gamble with your future like this. He's a wolf in sheep's clothing.

SECOND ANGEL

Okay, don't say you weren't warned, Eve. If you can't hear now, you'll just have to feel it later. There's just no way around it.

**"Really? I'll be wiser and be"....
"Anything, even a god"**

# SCENE VII

(Meanwhile, Adam continues caring for the animals; he is very happy, singing while he works.)


THIRD ANGEL

Dude, get moving! Go find your wife, 'cause she is making a deal with the devil.


ADAM

(Thinking about what to do, he suddenly stops to look up at the sky; seeing the sun's position, he knows it's getting late.)

Well, I'd better go and find my Eve. It's getting late.
(Chuckles.)

She is so easily missed.

(Starts to look for Eve.)

# SCENE VIII

(Back on the other side of the garden; Serpent interrupts Eve's fantasy.)


SERPENT

Come on, don't you want to be you own boss?


EVE
(Puzzled.)

I don't know. … What do you mean?


SERPENT

Do you really want to have someone else calling the shots when you can think for yourself? That's no fun!


FIRST ANGEL
(To Eve.)

Tell him that's none of his business.


EVE

Well, we're quite content with the way things are.


SECOND ANGEL
(Pleased with Eve.)

That's my girl! You are very satisfied. Now get away from the danger—*please!*


SERPENT
(Disappointed, but not giving up. Attempts to be more cunning.)

Really? You just want to settle? Can't you see that He just wants to keep you locked away in this garden … forever. Is this what you want? Don't you want to go out to see what happens elsewhere?


EVE

Elsewhere? I could leave?

SERPENT
(Pleased.)
Sure! No need to stay in this bubble; there's so much to see outside of here.

EVE
(Intrigued.)
Really?

SERPENT
Of course! Don't deprive yourself. … Come on, just try it; you'll see what I'm talking about.

FIRST ANGEL
No, Eve! Think about it—someone is lying to you, and it's certainly not God.

SECOND ANGEL
Eve, it's not too late to turn away.

EVE
(Picks the fruit.)

BOTH ANGELS
(Hide their faces in dismay.)
No-o-o-o-o-o!

EVE
(Bites into the fruit.)

FIRST ANGEL
(Removes hand from face to see Eve eating; extremely disappointed.)
Oh no! She didn't!

SECOND ANGEL
(Also disappointed; sad.)
Oh yes … she did! And we tried so hard to save her.

EVE
*Mmmm!* It does taste good.

SERPENT

See ... it's to die for!

EVE
(Gasps with fright as she looks at Serpent.)

SERPENT
(Chuckles.)

(Reassuringly.)

Oh, relax, Eve!

It's just my favorite expression.

EVE
(Relieved; smiles.)

SERPENT

That's better! Now take one to your husband, and make sure he eats it too.

EVE

Okay.

(Takes the fruit.)

It was delightful meeting you.

(Rushes to meet Adam.)

SERPENT

Oh, the pleasure was all mine! *Mmmm* ... ha, ha, h-a-a-a-a-a-a!

FIRST ANGEL

Master has got to be so disappointed in her.

SECOND ANGEL
(Shakes his head.)

His heart must indeed be sad.

# SCENE IX

(Eve meets Adam on the way. She is just skipping along, elated with the wonderful news. When she sees him, she stops; she does not make the fruit visible at this point.)

EVE

Adam! Oh, have I got a story to tell you! It's just unbelievable!

ADAM

There you are. Thank God! I was worried sick that you would get into trouble.

EVE

Who me? Oh no.

ADAM

Good! So, where have you been? What took you so long?

EVE

Traffic! Just kidding. Had an interesting encounter with a talking serpent. Can you imagine?

ADAM
(Very interested.)

Oh yeah?

(Angel arrives to help Adam.)

EVE
(Elated.)

Oh yeah! He told me the real truth about that tree that God told us not to partake of.

ADAM
(Alarmed and suspicious.)

Eve, what did this say?

EVE

He said that the part about us dying is a big piece of baloney.


ANGEL

(To Adam.)

Hey, I know she is your wife, but don't listen to anything she has to say.


ADAM

(Shrugs.)

Yeah, right, Eve … like you'd believe such nonsense.


ANGEL

Good job! You can get another wife, but there's only one life.


EVE

Well, yeah! He sounded so convincing that I actually ate the fruit.

(Shows him the fruit.)

And look at me, Adam! I'm still here—for real—I'm not a ghost.


ADAM

(Stands up, frantic; pulls his hair.)

Eve! … You did *what?!*

(Starts pacing back and forth.)

Oh my goodness! Oh boy! …

(Stops; looks at her, obviously distressed.)

What have you done? … Why? Why, Eve?! I never should have let you out of my sight.


EVE

(Unconcerned; thinks he is overreacting.)

Oh, just chill, Adam.


ADAM

(Shocked at her response, he pauses for a moment, staring at her regretfully.)

If I was with you, this would not have happened.


ANGEL

Right about that one!

EVE

(Excited.)

What are you worried about? It is delicious, and it will only make you wiser.


ADAM

(With sudden insight.)

Eve, this serpent must be that Satan we were warned about.


EVE

No way! Satan must be quite ugly and unattractive. This serpent was so cute and irresistible.


ADAM

(Walks away; he seems determined not to eat the fruit.)

Who gave you the authority to make the decision for both of us, anyway? Huh? I was just a shout away—why didn't you call me?


ANGEL

Adam, you have a mind of your own. … It's totally up to you.


EVE

(Matter-of-fact.)

Well, I didn't think that you would mind. Moreover, it just seemed too good a deal to pass up.


ANGEL

See what I'm talking about? This has trouble written all over it.


ADAM

(Upset.)

Do you know what this means?


EVE

Hey … what do you want me to do? What's done cannot be undone.


ADAM

Bingo! That's the big problem.


ANGEL

Move on, bro. … She's a goner!

**"Eve, you did what?"**
**"Well, whatever he said must be true."**

EVE
(Still trying to convince Adam.)
So? … What are you going to do? Are you going to eat it?

ADAM
(Thinking about it.)
Well … God will be dissatisfied with us.

EVE
(Boasting.)
Does he seem displeased with me?

ADAM
(Looks at Eve.)
Well … no …but—

EVE
(More confident; interrupts him.)

Okay, then!

ADAM
(Reconsiders; impassioned.)

Evita … you're putting me in a tough spot here. I don't want to disobey God, but … I don't want to displease you either.

EVE
(Seductively walks over to Adam and touches his face; pouts.)

Oh … Adamito! I never would have second thoughts about this if I were you.

ADAM
(Flattered.)

Really?

ANGEL

Yield not to temptation, Adam.

EVE

*R-e-a-l-l-y!*

(Hands the fruit to Adam; smiles.)

Eat?

ANGEL

If you'll just find the courage to say no, God will definitely provide a means of escape for you, Adam.

ADAM
(Takes the fruit, looks at it, and then turns to Eve.)

Hey, why worry? You are looking just fine to me.

EVE
(Teasingly models for him.)

See? … Picture of perfect health, right?
Death is not coming to this body anytime soon.
(Chuckles.)

ANGEL

Your looks are certainly deceiving you both.

ADAM

(Perks up, looking at Eve.)

Well, whatever that serpent said must be true, because you are still looking as innocent and beautiful as ever!

(Smiles and bites into the fruit; eyes light up.)

Wooh! I see what you're saying.

ANGEL

(Sad.)

I am so disappointed in you.

ADAM

(Still eating.)

This is really good stuff, Eve. You have a big surprise coming.

EVE

(Extremely satisfied.)

Told ya!

ANGEL

You have no idea what is good.

(Disappointed, but decides to stay.)

ADAM

So what else did the serpent say?

EVE

He says we can become whatever we want to be.

ADAM

No way! That's awesome!

EVE

Cool, eh?

ADAM

Yeah!


EVE

He also said that we can even leave the garden.


ADAM
(Extremely happy.)
Free as birds? It would be nice to see what's out there ... really.


ANGEL

Yeah, but it's a jungle out there and you'll have no one to care!


(Angel leaves.)


EVE
(Nods and smiles, looking at Adam.)
*R-e-a-l-l-y!*


BOTH
(Eve starts a chanting march; Adam follows.)
Freedom, choo-choo! Freedom, choo-choo! Freedom, choo-choo.


ADAM
(Stops; interrupting chanting march.)
But, Eve, how are we going to get out of here, anyway?


EVE
(Thinking.)
Ah! ... Don't worry; we'll find out soon.


BOTH
(Continuing chanting march.)
Freedom, choo-choo! Freedom, choo-choo!

ADAM
(Stops again; holds his head and then slides his hands down to his chest and trunk.)

Aaahhh … I feel funny.

(Adam takes off his white gown to expose his nakedness [body suit].)

EVE
(Stops; points to her head while smiling.)

Me too! We're probably getting wiser.

(Eve removes her gown also.)

ADAM
(Opens his eyes, looks at Eve, looks at himself, and then looks at Eve again; cries out in shock.)

Goodness! Are you seeing what I am seeing?

EVE
(Looks at herself and then at him.)

Oh no! We're naked!

ADAM
(Embarrassed.)

Let's find some covering

(They both run offstage.)

# SCENE X

(They return onstage with the leaves covering their pubic regions and buttocks, and Eve's chest.)

ADAM
(Very upset.)
Nice going, missy! I knew I shouldn't have trusted you.

EVE
(Annoyed.)
Oh Adam!

ADAM
I told you not to go anywhere without me, and God told you not to eat from that tree, but you just had to have your way. See what happens when you don't listen?

EVE
(Now frustrated with Adam, she wags her index finger at him and walks away from him.)
Don't you start with me now, mister!

ADAM
(Follows her.)
And you brought back that poison to me, and—

EVE
(Turns around; interrupts.)
And you *chose* to eat it … so stop whining.

ADAM
(Looks at her for a moment; starts pacing back and forth, looking confused and extremely nervous.)
Oh no! What are we going to do? God is going to be so mad at us.

                    EVE
                    (Boastful.)

No, he won't. He is such a sweet and gentle God. … He won't do a thing. Can't you see He just wanted to scare us … a little? … Don't worry about it.


                    ADAM
                    (Regretful.)

Come on, Eve … after what we did? No means no. We chose Satan over God!
                    (Pauses, thinking.)
You really think He won't be mad?


                    EVE
                    (Unrepentant.)

Sure. Listen, who else is here to care for the garden and the animals? Moreover, do you really think that after He put so much effort into making us, He would just get rid of us?


                    ADAM
                    (Distressed.)

Well, you have a point there, but we disobeyed Him; I don't think He's going to be happy with us.


                    EVE
                    (Irritated.)

Adam, you're too negative.
                    (Snaps her fingers at him.)
Snap out of it! … Focus.


                    ADAM
                    (Brightens up a bit.)


                    EVE
                    (Smiles.)

Good!
                    (Walking while thinking.)
Okay, we can try to persuade Him. … I know it works.


                    ADAM

And if that docsn't work?

EVE
(Bragging.)

Well, what you know what they say, three strikes and you are out. Hey, this is our first offense, so no big deal. Maybe we'll get a stern warning or a slap on the wrist; or, worst-case scenario—probation.

GOD
(Hidden; voice offstage throughout scene.)

Adam?

EVE
(Clings to Adam; scared.)

ADAM
(Tries to push her away.)

BOTH
(Try to hide.)

GOD

… Adam, where are you?

ADAM

Here we are, Lord.

GOD

Why are you hiding?

ADAM

We heard Your voice and were afraid.

GOD

Afraid? Oh Adam! Why did you do it? You ate of that fruit I forbid you to eat … didn't you?

ADAM

Yes, Lord, but …

(Points to Eve.)

… This never would have happened if You had not given this woman to me; she is the reason I ate it.

EVE
(Upset; turns away from Adam.)

GOD
Oh, so now she's "this woman". I thought she "completes" you.

ADAM
Well, it's true I said that, but I never knew she was going to be so much trouble!

GOD
Adam, you know better. You noticed I made you into a man and not a baby, didn't you? So, which part of "no" didn't you understand? Moreover, you have a brain—at least, I know I *gave* you one … why didn't you use it?!

EVE
(Laughs at Adam.)

ADAM
(Ashamed.)

Lord, are You mad at me?

GOD

Oh no … I never get mad. …

EVE
(To Adam.)

Told ya!

GOD

… I am just very disappointed. … Eve?

EVE
(Smiles.)

Yes, Lord?

GOD

What happened?

EVE

(Sly.)

Lord, I know You said not to eat the fruit, but it was so enticing.

(Blames Serpent.)

However, I was only admiring it until the serpent got my attention. You know how *he* is!


GOD

Oh, yes, indeed I do.


EVE

(Relieved; thinks she will not be punished.)

Great! Then You know how convincing and irresistible he can be. You are such a loving and patient God; I knew You would understand.


GOD

Oh, Eve, I do understand.


EVE

(Eyes light up, she is happy; looks at Adam, winks, him and gives him the thumbs-up.)


GOD

You defied me. … Actions speak louder than words. Much louder.


EVE

(Hangs her head in shame.)


ADAM

Lord, we are so sorry.


GOD

Me too. See, I tried to withhold the evil, and give only the good to you, but you allowed curiosity to get the best of you, so go ahead; do as you wish. … Eat as much as you like from that tree. …


BOTH

(Very surprised and happy; start smiling and dancing.)

GOD

… Knock yourselves out, *but* be prepared also to suffer the disappointments, grief, pain, and death that come with knowledge of good and evil.

BOTH

(Now shocked and disappointed.)

EVE

(Sulking.)

But why, God? Why did You leave the serpent here with us? You know how sly and dangerous he is.

GOD

Yes, I do. … But I want to honor your rights … your rights to choose whom you will worship.

EVE

(Regretful.)

It's not fair; he *made* me do it.

GOD

Really? So, he picked the fruit, gave it to you, and then forced you to eat it?

EVE

No … but …

GOD

Oh, so you made the decision to eat the fruit. It was your choice!

EVE

Well … ah …

(Searches for more excuses but is unable to find any.)

GOD

I do not compel anyone to respect Me; neither does he. If you love Me, you will obey Me. … It is that simple.

BOTH

(Hang their heads in shame.)

ADAM
(Impassioned.)

But, Lord, we love You!

GOD

No you don't. You do not disappoint and defy and hurt the one you love.

BOTH
(Stand silent, still hanging their heads in shame.)

GOD

Sorry … you failed the test. It pains my heart to do this, but it's time for some tough love. Because you chose to disobey Me, this is your punishment.
(Stern; cites Genesis 3:17, 19.)
"Cursed is the ground for thy sake; in sorrow shalt thou live all the days of thy life …. till thou return unto the ground; … For dust thou art, and unto dust shalt thou return."

ADAM

Lord, what do You mean?

GOD

It means that you're out of here. Yes, you wanted freedom. … It is here!

EVE
(Complacent.)

God, can You just give us a couple of minutes to pack a few things?

GOD
(Ignores her.)

(Angel of Death guides them out of the garden and stands at the gate. Eve sulks.)

ADAM
(Holds Eve by the hand while they leave garden; both are upset. Their new environment is harsh and ugly in contrast to the lush and beautiful garden.)

Come on. … See what you've done to us? Life was so good, but you just had to go mess it up.

**"Cursed is the ground for thy sake;
in sorrow shalt thou live all the days of thy life ....
till thou return unto the ground; .....:
For dust thou art, and unto dust shalt thou return."**

EVE
(Defensive; lets go of his hand.)
Hey, you're not totally blameless, you know!
(Nods her head.)
Yeah, sure—blame me; I'll probably get blamed for every problem after this too.

ADAM
(Walks away from her and the garden, shaking his head in disbelief; looks back at the garden and then at Eve.)
Do you really realize what just happened?

EVE
(Irritated.)
Duh!!!! We just got evicted!

ADAM
(Rolls his eyes.)
Well, yeah … but what I meant was that we allowed ourselves to be deceived by Satan—an outcast—and now we are homeless just like he is.

EVE
(Sadly agrees.)
And our future is doomed.

ADAM
You know what else happened? I used to care for the garden and the animals; now I don't even have a job!

EVE
And it's not as if we were not forewarned.
(Touches Adam on the shoulder.)
Oh … Adam! What are we going to do?

ADAM
(Shrugs his shoulders; looks despondent.)
I don't know. We are hungry, we have no home. …

EVE
(Also looks hopeless.)
And we don't even know where to go, since it's the first time we're crossing the border.

(They both sit down with elbows on knees and heads in hands for a few moments.)

ADAM
(Gets up and starts pacing, while shaking his head; talks to audience/congregation.)
Fairy tales, fairy tales—that's all the serpent's words were. We took the bait; we believed the fairy tale that the grass was greener on the other side. Well, now we know that it's not true. It was much, much greener in there.

(Points to garden.)

EVE
Well, it's too late!

ADAM
(Still pointing to the garden.)
We had it all, and we lost it all.

EVE
We are on death row.

(Opens hands.)
Now … we have nothing.

ADAM
Satan made us believe that we would gain big by disobeying God and breaking His law.
(Clenches his fist.)
Satan just wanted us to be miserable like he is—and it's working!

EVE
(Remorseful.)
Yep, never trust a snake!

(Cites Proverbs 14:12.)
"There is a way that seemeth right to a man but the end thereof are the ways of death."
(Shakes her head.)
Look at us! Boy … have we learned our lesson.

ADAM
(Swings his thumb jokingly at Eve but does not look at her.)

Oh, yes, Eve—be careful of the friends you keep, because they could lead you astray.

EVE
(Notices his actions; smiles.)

Hey, I saw that! … Be cautious when talking to strangers next time, and remember that sin comes in all forms; it can disguise itself as beauty.

ADAM

Most important, remember that if you don't obey there's a price to pay. The wages of sin is death.

EVE

We cannot serve two masters; for God, it's either all or nothing.
(She looks at Adam.)

Oh Adam, if you only knew.

ADAM

Yeah, Eve … and if you'd only listened.

BOTH
(Both heave a big sigh.)

If only we'd obeyed!

**THE END**

# 5

# Treasured Up and Ready To Go

## Recognizing the Importance of
## Stewardship and Thanksgiving

"But a certain man named Ananias, with Sapphira his wife, sold a possession,
And kept back [part] of the price, his wife also being privy [to it], and brought a
certain part, and laid [it] at the apostles' feet.
But Peter said, Ananias, why hath Satan filled thine heart to lie to the Holy Ghost,
and to keep back [part] of the price of the land?
Then Peter said unto her, How is it that ye have agreed together to tempt the Spirit
of the Lord?" (Acts 5:1–11)

"And he said unto them, Take heed, and beware of covetousness....
And he spake a parable unto them, saying, The ground of a certain rich man
brought forth plentifully, And he thought within himself, saying, What shall I
do?......
And he said, This will I do: I will pull down my barns, and build greater; and
there will I bestow all my fruits and my goods.
And I will say to my soul, Soul, thou hast much goods laid up for many years;
take thine ease, eat, drink, [and] be merry.
But God said unto him, [Thou] fool, this night thy soul shall be required of thee:
then whose shall those things be, which thou hast provided?" (Luke 12:15–20).

God blesses us in various ways, and sometimes our wealth depicts just that. As individuals, we
sometimes do not know how to handle our success and therefore become rather selfish. This play
is about stewardship and thanksgiving; it shows how some individuals react to their treasured
possessions.

# CHARACTERS

SIS. JOY        Scheming wife; easily swayed by worldly riches.

BRO. TOM     Deceptive husband.

SIS. PATSY    Christian; Sis. Joy's exercise partner (could be substituted with a male [renamed Bro. Patsy], who would be her trainer instead).

MR. JOHN     A selfish man who hoards his wealth.

# SETTING

Sis. Joy is at home getting ready for her evening workout/walk. Her husband, Bro. Tom, comes home from work with exciting news.

Mr. John is in front of his barn, overwhelmed by the yield of his crop.

Mr. John's house is across from Sis. Patsy's, and down the road from Sis. Joy and Bro. Tom's house. The sound of sirens and the glare of bright, flashing lights awaken them.

# TIME

Evening and late evening, early October 2006.
Early morning, August 2008.

# SCENE I

(Sis Joy is sitting on the couch, dressed in her exercise outfit. She starts to lace up her sneakers, preparing to go walking. Her husband, Bro. Tom, walks in.)

BRO. TOM
(Very excited.)
Sweetheart, I have some good news for you!

SIS. JOY
Oh yeah?

BRO. TOM
Remember the pledge we made at the end of the last harvest season—to give all the proceeds of the land sale for harvest this year?

SIS. JOY
(Finishes lacing up her sneakers, looks up, and answers slowly.)
Y-e-e-e-es. ...

BRO. TOM
(Thrilled.)
Well, it's way more than I expected—maybe up to four times more.

SIS. JOY
(With a big smile.)
Really?

BRO. TOM
You have a twinkle in your eye! ... *Hmmm* ... are you thinking what I'm thinking?

SIS. JOY
(Slyly.)
Let's see ... just give a portion and then keep the rest for ourselves?

BRO. TOM
(Very happy.)

Hey, great minds really do think alike!


SIS. JOY

And since the price of land is appreciating so much, we'll just leave it there—in a couple of years it should triple again.

(Daydreaming.)

Wow! What an investment!


BRO. TOM

So, if anyone asks about it, we can't tell them the truth—right?

**"Great minds really do think alike"**

SIS. JOY

Of course!

(Chuckles.)

They won't be able to handle the truth.


BRO. TOM

(Fantasizing.)

So, in a few years we could sell, and then we could use the money to go on vacation, buy some new wheels. …


SIS. JOY

(Looks at him, smiling slyly.)

Or redo the kitchen.


BRO. TOM

Or open an investment account! We can treat ourselves; the possibilities are endless!


SIS. JOY

(Looks at her watch.)

Oops, it's getting late; I must go for my walk before eight.

(Takes a deep breath.)

*Mmmm,* fresh air! Sometimes the best things in life really are free.

(Chuckles.)


BRO. TOM

(Playfully warns her.)

Remember: don't ask, don't tell!


SIS. JOY

Oh, please—whatever happens in this house, stays in this house.

(She winks at him as she turns and leaves.)


BRO. TOM

(Happily, to himself.)

Wow! The future is looking extremely bright … yeah!

# SCENE II

(Sis. Patsy has started her walk because Sis. Joy is a little late. Sis. Patsy stops to talk to Mr. John, a neighbor.)

SIS. PATSY

Hey there, John, how are you?

MR. JOHN
(Stands in the midst of numerous baskets of fruits and vegetables; appears frustrated.)

Great, wonderful, ecstatic; but I'm faced with a dilemma.

SIS. PATSY
(Puzzled, but willing to help.)

Okay … what's the problem?

MR. JOHN
(Spreads hands to indicate his produce.)

See, all this? I got way more than I am prepared for. My crop was so plentiful that I have nowhere to store it all.
(Pauses, shaking his head.)

And I am not even through with the harvesting.

SIS. PATSY
(Relieved; smiles.)

Sounds like a pleasant problem to me.

MR. JOHN
(Still a little distressed.)

I agree; but, still, what do I do?

SIS. PATSY
(Counsels him.)

Aren't you aware of your surroundings? Come on—there are so many people that you could help with just a small portion of this harvest.

**"What can I do?  My barn is already full"**

**"Aaah! I will retire early and take it easy for the rest of my life"**

MR. JOHN
(Sarcastic.)
Oh, I see … I work my fields to support the community.

SIS. PATSY
(Apologetic.)
No, that's not what I meant. Please don't interpret it that way.

MR. JOHN
(Upset.)
Well, I'm not the one who told them not to work hard and not to succeed! Why should they gain from my pain?

SIS. PATSY
(Calmly.)
Come on now, John. Remember what Luke 6:38 tells us: "Give and it will be given to you. A good measure, pressed down, shaken together and running over, will be poured into your lap. For with the measure you use, it will be measured to you."

MR. JOHN
(Doubtful.)
But then what will I have left for tomorrow?

SIS. PATSY
(Smiling, cites Matthew 6:34.)
"No need to worry about tomorrow."

MR. JOHN
(Shocked.)
Oh, I can see you don't; it shows!
(Forthright.)
Well, Mr. Rainy Day can arrive at any time …
(Slowly)
So, I … am … preparing!

(Sis. Joy walks up.)

SIS. JOY
There you are, Sis. Patsy. Are we ready to walk?

SIS. PATSY

Not just yet. John has a problem with his harvest.
>(Rolls her eyes.)

It's too bountiful; can you give him some healthy ideas as to what he can do with it?

SIS. JOY

Well, sure!
>(Turns to Mr. John.)

How about you give some away to—

SIS. PATSY
>(Interrupts, clearing her throat.)

Nope! We've already been there.

SIS. JOY
>(Pauses; looks at Sis. Patsy, who raises an eyebrow; turns
>back to Mr. John.)

Okay, then, John … let's see … *hmmm,* how about you come to our church? You could join in the harvest festivities.

# MR. JOHN
>(Suspicious.)

And what does going to *your* church have to do with *my* crop?

SIS. JOY
>(Cites Proverbs 3:9, 10.)

Well, the Bible says, "Honor the LORD with thy substance, and with the firstfruits of all thine increase: So shall thy barns be filled with plenty, and thy presses shall burst out with new wine."

MR. JOHN
>(Bluntly.)

And your point is?

SIS. JOY

When we show God that we really appreciate His gifts, He blesses us even more, so that we will continue to honor Him.

SIS. PATSY
(Smiles, turning to Mr. John.)
Yeah, I know … yours is already full and overflowing, but you don't want it to become empty, right?

MR. JOHN
(Reluctantly gives in.)
Okay, when is it?

SIS. PATSY
Next Sunday at 2 p.m. If you need help bringing your produce, let me know.

MR. JOHN
(Excited.)
I can sell my stuff there?

SIS. JOY
(Happy for him.)
Yes, of course!

MR. JOHN
(Excited.)
Great!

SIS. PATSY
(Interjects.)
You realize that the proceeds will go to the church.

MR. JOHN
(Angry.)
What?! *I* don't get the money for what *I* sell?

SIS. PATSY
(Calmly.)
John, the whole point is that it's a thanksgiving gift—to God.

MR. JOHN
(Adamant; shakes his head.)
No way, Jose. I'm not giving away my stuff like that.

SIS. JOY
(Surprised.)

You're not going to—

MR. JOHN
(Folds his arms across his chest, scowling.)

Nope!

SIS. PATSY

Not even to church—to God?

MR. JOHN

Unh-uh.

SIS. JOY

Well, that's really sad, John, because if God did not want you to have that crop, no matter how hard you worked, it would not be yours.

MR. JOHN
(Defiant.)

Oh, really? Is that so?

SIS. PATSY

Yes. Isn't it God who puts life in the seed and power in the soil—giving the crop rain and sunshine so everything would grow?

MR. JOHN
(Quiet; thinking.)

Well … if you put it that way, yes.

(Rebellious and arrogant again.)

But it's mine now!

SIS. JOY
(Trying to convince him.)

Your blessings come from God, John—even you don't deserve them. Have you ever considered what would have happened if there had been a tornado or a flood or some other disaster?

### MR. JOHN
(Cynical.)

Yes! And that's why I cannot just give away my stuff; never know *what* might happen.

### SIS. JOY
(Disappointed.)

I wish you would be a faithful steward.

### MR. JOHN

A what?

### SIS. PATSY

A steward—someone who is put in charge of something for someone else. In this case, you are God's steward, because it's His crop and He just left you to supervise it for Him. Unfortunately, you don't see it that way.

(Rebukes him, pointing at him with her index finger.)

You need to be loyal and accountable to Him!

### MR. JOHN
(Upset; turns to walk away.)

Enough already!

(Turns back, chastising them.)

I know my Bible too! Ecclesiastes 9:10 says, I have found something to do with my hands, and I have done it with all my might. This is my reward, so can I please enjoy it the way I want to?

### SIS. JOY
(Clears her throat.)

And how do you plan to do that?

### MR. JOHN
(Relaxes; now very confident.)

Well, I have an idea. I've heard about this new type of fuel made from corn; maybe I'll just contact one of those big companies and unload my surplus on them.

### SIS. PATSY
(Sarcastic.)

Oh yeah!

MR. JOHN

Yes, and then I'll invest in one of those companies with high-yield returns. After that, I'll just take it easy. …

(Fantasizing.)

For the rest of my life, maybe—oh … the future is going to be so bright!

SIS. JOY

(Very interested.)

Early retirement?

MR. JOHN

You got it!

(Mocking them.)

Be honest, isn't that everyone's dream? To go see the world—eat, drink, entertain, and have fun, fun … and more fun!

SIS. JOY

(Liking what she hears, she starts to fantasize too.)

That sounds so exciting!

SIS. PATSY

(Clears her throat, gives Sis. Joy an unpleasant look at her sudden change of tune.)

SIS. JOY

(Composes herself.)

But … how rewarding will that be, John?

SIS. PATSY

(To Mr. John.)

Yes! You sound so positive that all will go your way.

MR. JOHN

(Bragging.)

I am positive.

(Looks first at Sis. Patsy, and then at Sis. Joy.)

I'm blessed.

SIS. JOY

(Annoyed; cites Luke 12:21.)

You are? Ha! The one who is truly blessed is the one who is rich toward God.


MR. JOHN

(Offended.)

Well, don't disrespect me! Exactly what would you call this?

(Extends arm to indicate his crop.)


SIS PATSY

(Tries to give him a reality check.)

Do you really want to set up your treasures on this earth, with pain and fear—and recessions and depressions?


SIS. JOY

(Nods.)

That's right. You will only leave everything behind, and who will enjoy it then?

(Laughs.)

Instead, you could send your luggage ahead—straight to heaven—by helping others; and then you will be rich in the sight of God, and your ultimate gift will be eternal life.


MR. JOHN

(Still not convinced.)

Hey, I cannot give away surety for uncertainty. You know what they say, keep your friends close; but I say, keep your possessions closer.

(Winks at them, giving them the thumbs-up.)


SIS. PATSY

(To Sis. Joy.)

Well, I think it's time for us to go, because you know what they also say, sow your seed the way you know best, and the Holy Spirit will do the rest.

(Laughs, turning to Mr. John.)

Have a nice evening, John.


(Leaving Mr. John; they start walk.)

SIS. JOY

(Thoughtfully.)

You know what the problem with John is?

(Cites Matthew 6:33.)

".... Seek ye first the kingdom of God, and his righteousness; and all these things shall be added unto you."

(Shakes her head sadly.)

He has all he ever wanted, so he has stopped seeking.

SIS. PATSY

(Agreeing.)

Yes, that is so sad.

(Appears distressed.)

You know, every time harvest comes around, I think of the rich fool; John is just like him.

SIS. JOY

Oh yes! How could I forget that greedy man? John is just like him.

(Smiles, shaking her head.)

SIS. PATSY

… And the couple that tried to break their pledge with God; harvest reminds me of them too.

SIS. JOY

(Shocked; her eyes pop out; she cannot speak.)

SIS. PATSY

What're their names again?

SIS. JOY

(She appears troubled and lost in thought.)

Huh?

SIS. PATSY

(A bit puzzled; repeats her comment.)

The couple that broke their pledge with God; they sold the land and then lied about the sale price—just because they wanted to keep some of the money.

(Stops; looks at Sis. Joy.)

SIS. JOY
(Avoids eye contact with Sis. Patsy; attempts to walk away.)

SIS. PATSY
(Suddenly remembering.)

Ananias and Sapphira! How could I have forgotten. … Well, the Boss will repossess his stuff whenever He feels like it, so —

SIS. JOY
(Scared; interrupts tersely.)

Yes, I know.

(Still trying to hurry off; afraid her guilt and shame will betray her to Sister Patsy.)

SIS. PATSY
(Tries to keep up with Sis. Joy.)

I know we all have our faults, but there are some things I know you and I would never do.

SIS. JOY
(Ashamed; turns her head away; stammers.)

'C–course not!

SIS. PATSY

Well, we did more talking than walking today, so tomorrow it will be twice the work! See you, Joy. …

SIS. JOY
(Gives a good-bye wave without looking at Sis. Patsy.)

(Both go home.)

# SCENE III

(Sis. Joy enters the house, frantic about what she and Sis. Patsy just discussed. Bro. Tom relaxes on the couch; he looks up when Sis. Joy comes in.)

SIS. JOY
(Distraught.)

Honey … we are going down!

BRO. TOM
(Very surprised.)

What? What are you talking about?

SIS. JOY

We are going down, 'cause we've been playing around.

BRO. TOM
(Still clueless, attempts to be funny.)

We—or you?

SIS. JOY
(Irritated; rolls her eyes.)

That pledge we made!

(Pauses; visibly upset.)

We are going to have to honor it.

BRO. TOM
(Sits up straight, suddenly attentive.)

Okay, Joy—who were you just talking to?

SIS. JOY

The neighbors—Patsy … John—why?

BRO. TOM
(A little disappointed.)

You mentioned it, didn't you?

SIS. JOY

No! … Of course not! We have a "don't ask, don't tell" agreement about that, right?

BRO. TOM

Right! So … what happened?

(Pauses, puzzled.)

Why are you so upset all of a sudden?

SIS. JOY

(Sighs.)

Remember that couple from the Bible—Ananias and Sapphira—who lied in a way that is similar to what we are about to do? And then they both dropped dead in the church! *Poof!*

BRO. TOM

(Rolls his eyes, mocking her.)

Oh, come on, Joy! Do you really believe that fairy tale? If you ask me, it sounds like some ancient, religious soap opera.

SIS. JOY

Well, do you believe everything in the Bible?

BRO. TOM

Of course I do! How could you even ask such a question?

SIS. JOY

(Distressed.)

If you believe everything in the Bible, why don't you believe this? I do not want my soul to be lost, Tom!

(Pauses, shaking her head; speaks in a gentler tone.)

Honey, we could go out with a real bang, but I do not want all that drama.

BRO. TOM

(Still making light of the situation.)

What's the difference for me? … I have to face it every day.

(Smiling while looking at her, because he is referring to her.)

SIS. JOY

(Upset.)

Stop kidding around! This is very serious.

> (Takes a deep breath; calms down a bit and then sits beside him on the couch; takes his hands in hers.)

We covet, we steal, and we lie to God. God does not like dishonesty!

BRO. TOM

(Defensive; pulls his hands from hers; stands up.)

So now we are coveting what is ours?

SIS. JOY

Oh Tom! Let's not go there. You know what I mean.

> (She is tired of trying to convince him.)

Okay. I do not want to be left out of the heavenly zone, so—

> (Pauses; takes a good look at him.)

You're on your own.

> (Gets up to leave).

BRO. TOM

(Tries to stop her; cajoling.)

Okay, darling, you're right. It really was a terrible idea.

> (Reflective.)

Just goes to show you that Christians are also affected by greed.

> (Looks up.)

Lord, please forgive us. Create in us a clean heart, and renew a right spirit within us.

# SCENE IV

(Bro. Tom and Sis. Joy walk outside after hearing emergency vehicles in the early morning hours. Sis. Patsy is already there.)

SIS. JOY
(Confused; watches the ambulance leave.)
Police? Ambulance? What happened here, Patsy?

SIS. PATSY
(Reflective and sad.)
The clock stopped on Mr. John.

BRO. TOM
(Surprised.)
Really? He seemed so healthy!

SIS. PATSY
Yeah … he must have died from a broken heart—and more.

BRO. TOM
How so?

SIS. JOY
Oh … darling, I forgot to tell you. Turns out, John changed his plans; he invested most of his money with an old man who scammed it all in some crazy scheme. The rest of it was invested in that money market that crashed recently.

BRO. TOM
(Solemn, but touched.)
So he took it to heart, eh? Bowed out, rather than living in a little discomfort.
(Shakes his head sadly.)
Life is so much more than the "abundance of possessions."

SIS. JOY
(Also sad.)

Sad, isn't it? Nothing is wrong with having possessions, but when one puts security into life and leaves God out of it, that is just a lose-lose situation.

SIS. PATSY
(Agrees.)

Poor John. He just made plans for his time here, forgetting about eternity. … I certainly did not see a trailer following that hearse.

SIS. JOY
(Offers sobering advice from Proverbs 11:24.)

We have to spread the word that when we are blessed by God, we are not to hoard our wealth, but instead try to bless other lives with it. After all, the more we give the richer we'll become.

BRO. TOM
(Thinking.)

*Hmmm* … I have to reexamine that point, 'cause ever since I can remember, my father has been giving away—whatever he could find—and he is still a poor man.

SIS. JOY

Ah! Luke 16: 9 says, "Use worldly wealth to gain friends for yourselves, so that when it is gone, you will be welcomed into eternal dwellings."

BRO. TOM
(Edified.)

Okay! Smart man. He is storing up his treasures in heaven. So, he might look like a poor man to me, but indeed he is rich toward God.

SIS. PATSY
(Nods.)

Yes.

(Distressed.)

I'm so sorry that we could not get through to John; I feel like we just wasted our time with him.

SIS. JOY
(Very grateful for the second chance that she and Bro.
Tom received.)

Don't say that, Patsy—stop beating upon yourself. Your job is to continue to sow your own seeds, and water them whenever you can, because you never know how the crop will turn out. …
(Pauses; looks at her husband, smiles, and then looks back at Sis. Patsy.)

Just trust me on that one!

SIS. PATSY
(Perplexed.)

How can you be so sure, Joy? The man took his life!

BRO. TOM
(Very reassuring; to Sis. Patsy.)

Sister, our efforts are never in vain, regardless of how it seems. We need to store up our treasures in heaven by investing in people, because they are the only "things" we can take with us … to heaven.

SIS. JOY
(Smiling; cites Luke 12:34.)

Yes—"where your treasure is, there will your heart be also"!

**THE END**